"Just what the hell do you think you're doing, Helm? You're a fugitive from justice. You must know you can't possibly get away with . . ."

I sighed wearily. "The last man who told me what I couldn't get away with got a nice, sharp knife inserted into his anatomy, all the way. Don't tempt me. This trigger pulls real easy."

I went on, "After you've worked things out, you'll understand why I'm not about to let myself be arrested. Roger submitted to you, knowing he was innocent and figuring he'd be able to prove it; now he's dead. Anybody who thinks I'm going to forget that little object lesson has got his head screwed on backwards. If you boys want me, you're going to have to take me. Roger cost you three or four men. I'm better than he was, if I do say so myself. I'm older, uglier, smarter, tougher, and meaner. . . ."

● ●

Fawcett Gold Medal Books
by Donald Hamilton:

the retaliators

donald hamilton

a fawcett gold medal book

fawcett publications, inc., greenwich, connecticut

the retaliators

••

one ....

I was unexpectedly rich and I didn't like it.

I stood in the gleaming, modern lobby of the New Mexico National Bank in my home town of Santa Fe—well, it's as much of a home town as anybody has in my line of work. I used to live there once is what I really meant to say, and I come back occasionally because I happen to like the place.

I looked at the two paper items handed me by the bank teller. One was a draft in my name made out to the Southwest Motor Company, the local Chevrolet agency, in the amount of eight thousand five hundred and seven dollars and forty-two cents. Even these inflated days, it seemed like a lot of money to pay for a vehicle that wasn't a Rolls or Mercedes—a truck, yet! —but what the hell, I could afford it. A single man earning danger pay who spends most of his time traveling on government business and a government expense account finds that the stuff tends to pile up faster than he can get rid of it during his brief periods of leave. In addition to this account in Santa Fe I had another in Washington, D.C., plus some conservative investments running to pleasantly substantial figures.

Up to this morning, the money had been a source of some comfort to me. Its existence had assured me that if I got myself badly shot up or otherwise damaged in the line of duty, I wouldn't have to starve on a government pension. Now I wasn't quite so happy about my financial status. As I said, I was rich. Unexpectedly so.

I looked at the second object handed me by the pretty Spanish-American girl at the window marked SAVINGS: my bankbook. When I'd brought it in, it had showed a balance just large enough to cover the purchase I proposed to make, with a few hundred to spare. However, the girl had spent some time bringing it up to date. She'd added the interest that had accumulated since my last visit over a year ago. She'd also discovered a deposit made last week, unrecorded in the book. When she'd got through adding and subtracting, instead of being practically broke here as I'd expected, I found that I was still, even after my sizable withdrawal, the proud owner of twenty thousand six hundred and thirty-one dollars and some cents.

Very nice. It isn't every government employee who can go around making twenty-grand deposits in his savings account—except that I hadn't made the deposit.

I repeat, I hadn't been in Santa Fe for well over a year; and I hadn't sent anybody to deposit twenty big bills to my account, either. . . . I stood there for a moment, taking my time about folding the bank draft and putting it away in my wallet. I'd had some reason to expect trouble, but I must confess I hadn't anticipated it would take this form. Somebody had obviously arranged an expensive deadfall for me. The question was, what did he expect me to do with the bait? And what kind of a heavy object would he drop on me when I did it?

Well, the answer to the last question was easy. To switch metaphors, you don't construct a handsome and costly frame without inviting folks to admire it, preferably folks with a certain amount of authority. Sooner or later I could expect to meet a gent with a badge, a self-righteous attitude, and a lot of nosy questions about that large and mysterious deposit, like who'd paid it to me for doing what, and just how did I reconcile taking a sizable bribe —as it appeared to be—with my duty to my employer, the United States of America.

It is, of course, one of the oldest of the standard TV gambits, just about as hoary as the one where the hero is arrested for murder because he picked up the gun lying beside the body, so naturally everybody assumes he did the shooting. Well, I ask you. If you walk in on a fresh corpse, what the hell are you supposed to do if you are packing no firearm of your own? Stand there unarmed, waiting for the lurking murderer to make you victim number two? Or grab the nearest weapon fast and to hell with fingerprints?

And then there's the ancient gag of slipping money into the bank in the name of somebody for whom you want to make a lot of trouble, and arranging it to look as if he took it for crooked or treasonable purposes. They still do it, and they still buy it, although a simple question to your friendly neighborhood banker will elicit the reluctant answer that there's really no serious obstacle to crediting money to another guy's savings as long as you know the account number and can spare the dough.

Well, to hell with that, for the moment. My mind was working very rapidly on one level, while on another I was surveying my surroundings and wondering sourly how anybody managed to get any work done in such a wide-open, goldfish-bowl of a place. Personally, I need peace and privacy when I'm going to perform a demanding intellectual task like counting money. I looked at the dark-haired girl behind the window and she didn't look so attractive any longer. I mean, goddamn it, what the hell kind of a financial institution was it that let the female help slouch around in pants with their shirttails out? All the girl needed was a pail and a scrub brush and she'd be all set to do a job on the floors. It was all part of the picture, I told myself irritably; if the employees were so sloppy about maintaining a businesslike appearance, no wonder they let folks wander in casually and stick large wads of cash into other folks' accounts.

Nobody seemed the least bit interested in me. I didn't take that too seriously. With twenty thousand dollars invested in me, he'd be interested, all right, whoever he was. . . .

Actually, I was debating with myself the advisability of taking the obvious, innocent route, loudly disclaiming any knowledge of the money right here and now, and demanding that my fouled-up account be straightened out immediately minus what didn't belong to me, since obviously the bank's computer had got the wrong Matthew L. Helm.

The plan had some attractive features. It didn't require much brainwork, for one thing. For another, it might get me an interview with the teller who'd accepted the deposit. However, I knew that after the week that had passed he, or she, would probably remember nothing about the depositor. Probably. There was, of course, a possibility that some odd little incident had occurred, or been made to occur, that had fixed the incident in the teller's memory. In that case, I was fairly certain, it would turn out that the money had been brought in by a skinny character considerably taller than average—a gent, now that the teller came to think of it, who'd looked pretty much like me.

The trouble was, I'd spent the last couple of months at the goddamned ranch in Arizona (we seldom refer to it without the adjective) where we go for retraining and repairs. I'd been having a little trouble with my shoulder, caused by some submachine gun bullets picked up in the line of duty—over in Europe, if it matters. When I'd finally got back to the U.S. that fall, I'd been informed that, strange though it might seem, my country could actually struggle along without my services temporarily. I'd been sentenced to sixty days of clean living and healthful therapy, mitigated by a month's leave afterwards. In a sense, therefore, I had the best alibi in the world. Numbers of professional-type government employees with spotless reputations, who'd supervised my reconditioning, could swear that last week I couldn't possibly have been depositing money in Santa Fe or anywhere else. There was just one catch. Officially, the ranch doesn't exist. We don't exist. Sometimes I think I don't exist. Certainly my job doesn't, officially.

So that was one alibi that would never be used; and I'm not the only guy six feet four in the country. Others can be hired; and there are such things as high-heeled boots and elevator shoes. After a week, your ordinary witness probably wouldn't remember more than one distinguishing feature of a stranger encountered in the day's work. If the body had been tall enough to be memorable, the teller would be unlikely to recall the face clearly enough to testify that it wasn't mine. That would leave me vulnerable. ("Is the defendant really asking this court to believe that he was *impersonated,* ha-ha? That an unknown individual resembling him closely, his twin brother from Australia, perhaps, generously presented him with twenty thousand unearned dollars—*twenty thousand,* ladies and gentlemen!—while he was engaged in some mysterious business he is not free to discuss, at a mysterious location he is not at liberty to reveal? The jury will, I am sure, draw its own conclusions. . . .")

The fact I had to keep clearly in mind was: you don't play poker with thousand-dollar chips in large quantities without first dealing yourself a pretty good hand. The direct and honest approach must have been anticipated. If

I tried to use it, I'd be playing the other man's game—whoever the other man was, and whatever his game might be.

Furthermore, at the moment my immediate concern wasn't what impression I might make on a hypothetical court of law convened at some unspecified time in the distant future. The essential thing, right now, was to preserve my freedom until I could consult Washington and see how matters stood and what I was supposed to do about them. I could feel the noose tightening around me as I hesitated, but I reminded myself that if I actually did wind up a fugitive, as seemed quite possible, I'd need money in large amounts, and it was only fair to let the opposition foot the bill.

"On second thought, Miss," I said, "I think I'd better get some cash, too. Could I have another withdrawal slip, please?"

A little while later, I stepped out onto the sidewalk in what I hoped was a casual and relaxed manner with ten grand of my unearned wealth—even this close to Texas, it hadn't seemed advisable to attract attention by asking for more mad-money than that—buttoned into the pocket of my shirt, a snug fit. They don't make hunting-shirt pockets the roomy way they used to; and it seems like a hell of a cheapskate way of saving wool. Outside, I checked to see if the Lincoln was still hanging around.

It was there all right, moving slowly around the Plaza as it waited for me, all dark blue and shiny, somebody's private two-door land yacht with the silly little peep-hole quarter windows currently fashionable. I frowned at it thoughtfully. Maybe I owed it, or its occupant, an apology. When I'd first spotted it tailing me a couple of days ago, I'd jumped to conclusions. There are a few people in the world who don't like me, and some of them are wealthy enough for Lincoln Continentals, or their governments are; but most of them are fairly direct fellows with single-track minds. If one of them ever decided I was worth going after, or got instructions to go after me, he'd come to kill, not to play games with my bank account.

Mr. Continental—or Mrs. Continental, or Miss Continental—was apparently a more devious type, assuming that he or she was actually responsible. There was, of course, a remote possibility that the surveillance here in Santa Fe had nothing to do with the financial finagling here in Santa Fe. I didn't really believe that, but I had to keep all possibilities in mind.

As you'll gather, I'd never got a good look at the occupant of the big coupe, not good enough for sex determination. The tinted windows of today's air-conditioned conveyances are great for privacy; men wear their hair just as long as women; there's often not even a hell of a big difference in dress; and I'd made a point of not looking too hard. Instead, after spotting my shadow, I'd gone about the business of outfitting myself for the special winter hunting season that was to open in a few days in a certain rugged area of the state.

I'd got the clothes and the boots and the rifle, and I'd tried to hire a four-wheel-drive vehicle and, failing that, had flipped and arranged to buy one. Actually, I'd already had some kind of winter boondocks excursion in mind when I'd come here from the ranch. Two months of that regimented life had put me in a mood to get off by myself for a while. I hadn't really planned on a hunting trip, however—considering my profession, that would have been kind of like an infantryman taking up backpacking in his spare time.

However, after realizing that I was being shadowed, I'd remembered the special season I'd read about, and made some calls to arrange for a permit. Anybody who wanted to come after me in wilderness terrain I knew pretty well, during a week when I could carry an accurate long-range rifle openly and legally in my hands, was welcome to do so. We'd get the whole thing settled on my terms in my kind of country—but now it seemed that I'd misread the situation completely. Well, nobody's right all the time.

I walked deliberately across the Plaza and went into a drug store and bought a big roll of one-inch adhesive tape and some other stuff. If Mr. Continental had scouts to tell him about it, he could have fun wondering what I was planning to stick to what.

There was a filling station around the corner, I recalled, with an outside phone booth. It was time to touch home base. I strolled down there and called Washington, using the emergency number. On that line, we don't use the fancy secret-agent ID routines prescribed in the manual. There often isn't time. I heard the ringing stop as the phone was picked up a couple of thousand miles away.

"Yes?" The voice was reassuringly familiar.

"Eric here," I said.

"Where are you, Matt?" asked the man we call Mac, for whom I'd worked most of my adult life.

I made a face at the traffic going by. He'd given me a warning signal by countering my code name with my real name—well, nickname. It said we didn't have the wire to ourselves. It was a blow, although one that wasn't entirely unexpected. But if even the emergency line wasn't safe, that meant news of the situation, whatever it was, had reached Washington, and the Internal Security people were already snooping around trying to get something on somebody, preferably me.

"Never mind the geography, sir," I said, glancing at my watch. "I've run into a little spot of trouble, as our British friends would say."

"I know all about your little trouble." Mac's voice was severe. "About forty thousand dollars' worth, isn't it?"

I whistled softly to myself. So my Washington account had been loaded, also. Somebody was playing rough.

"That's a nice round figure," I said. "Where did you hear it, sir?"

"Did you expect to get away with it forever?" Now the

voice over the phone was stern, and at the same time reproachful. "The head of the Bureau of Internal Security has been here, Andrew Euler himself. Following information received, his people have traced two large payments to you. The money has also been traced in the other direction. It originated, I'm told, with a gentleman currently calling himself Groening—our records refer to him as Gerber, or Gulick; he seems to like that initial—who's been under BIS surveillance for some time, Mr. Euler informs me. They've pulled him in and he's talking. Apparently he's been acting as paymaster for a nationwide network of spies and traitors; but of course you know that since you're one of them."

"Am I, sir?"

I watched a gleaming, dark blue coupe move down the street outside in a deliberate and dignified manner. It had Arizona license plates. It vanished around the corner.

"I do hope you're going to be sensible about this, Matt, now that your treasonable activities have been brought to light," Mac was saying. "You are certainly too intelligent to claim that you've been framed, as Roger did when they arrested him in Yuma a few days ago. You know how ridiculous that always sounds; and the description Mr. Euler has of the man who deposited money to both your accounts resembles you too closely for denials to carry much conviction. As for Norma's reaction, slipping across the Mexican border at Tijuana, that's hardly the act of an innocent person. It isn't likely that her investigation of Ernemann would have led her—or Roger either—to that desolate, dried-up sea bottom known as the great Southwest. As you're doubtless aware, Eric, Ernemann has never yet been known to set foot off city pavement in the line of business; dirty work in dark alleys is his specialty, remember?"

"Yes, sir," I said. "I remember."

He went on: "Nor is there any chance Norma could have been trying to establish liaison with a Mexican agent

in the line of duty, since our relations in that quarter—
you remember the fiasco of your assignment down there a
few years ago, the one involving flying saucers, for heav-
en's sake! —have deteriorated even further, and I've
strictly forbidden all such contacts. No, both Norma and
Roger must simply have been seeking sanctuary among
the Mexicans. . . . I believe it's proper to call them Mexicans if they live in Mexico, although I gather that people
of the same racial lineage insist on being called Spanish if
they live above the border. People are very sensitive
about such things these days, are they not, Eric?"

"Yes, sir," I said, listening closely.

"For instance," he went on, "you come from Swedish
ancestry, as I recall, but I doubt that you object stren-
uously to being called a Swede. I know a gentleman from
Denmark who's quite happy to be called a Dane. But a
citizen of Japan, of my acquaintance, becomes quite irate
if he is called a Jap. And then again, most male residents
of England refer to themselves as Englishmen. I've never
heard a French citizen object to being called a Frenchman. Yet a certain gentleman from China is said to consider Chinaman a very derogatory term. I must say I am
getting tired of catering to all these odd historical preju-
dices, aren't you, Eric?" He laughed shortly. "Of course
this is entirely beside the point. I must ask you to forgive
and forget this digression. The point, of course, is that I
must strongly advise you to give yourself up to Mr. Euler
or his representatives. You know that he has always been
a good friend of this organization; and that you can expect fair treatment from him, which, I must say, is more
than you really deserve after betraying. . . ."

I glanced at the second hand of my watch. It had
turned far enough, perhaps a little too far. It was time for
me to hang up and get out of there, not that it would
make much difference if the BIS people already had me
spotted—if, say, the cruising Lincoln was theirs. I didn't
really think it was, however. Andrew Euler, their boss,

was noted for two things: fanatic morality and penny-pinching economy. No employees of the Bureau of Internal Security dared to sleep with anyone to whom they weren't married, went the rumor; it was even said that a cocktail or cigarette could seriously damage your career in that outfit. Euler's paper-clip-counting parsimony was also legendary, making it unlikely that any of his people would employ a Lincoln for surveillance when a Volkswagen would do.

I replaced the phone gently, and drew a long breath as I stepped out of the booth. So far, so good. Considering the handicaps under which he was operating, Mac had given me as clear a briefing as I could have hoped for. . . .

"Please get in! Quickly!"

It was the Arizona Lincoln again, having made the tour around the block. The driver, who'd thrown open the curb door to address me, was a woman. One small mystery, at least, was resolved.

"They're waiting at your hotel!" she snapped. "They were asking for you at the desk. They'll arrest you if you go there. Get in, please, I'm blocking traffic!"

I didn't know her; but, although I keep trying, there are still some handsome ladies around with whom I'm not acquainted. At least I didn't know anything bad about her; and I'd already decided that the wheels she was driving made it unlikely she was working for government security or its straight-laced, tight-fisted chief. I got in.

two ....

She drove the big car badly. That is, she drove it timidly, like a graduate of one of those training schools that are the curse of the American highway; the ones that don't teach driving but something called "defensive driving," meaning that their students are brainwashed to believe that the sole purpose of putting a vehicle on the road is to get it back into the garage again unscratched, no matter how many people you obstruct or delay in the process. The idea that automobiles were invented to provide efficient and reasonably rapid transportation had obviously never occurred to her.

Resigning myself to this slow and fearful progress, I leaned forward a bit so I could study the view in the right-hand rear-view mirror while I organized in my mind the information I'd just received over the phone. Obviously, the situation in Washington was very difficult at the moment. Mac had had to go to elaborate lengths to transmit the data and instructions I needed without leaving himself open to a charge of aiding and abetting an employee suspected of treason. The reference to an investigation of a gent named Ernemann had been, of course, pure doubletalk. We don't investigate people. The government of the United States of America is lousy with investigators of one kind or another, but we're not among them. Our duties are somewhat different, and we don't discuss them over bugged telephones. Nevertheless, the orders had got through: I knew what to do and whom to do it to.

Beyond that, the key was Mac's deliberate statement that this Ernemann had never yet been known to set foot off city pavement in the line of business. Well, Ernemann was not well known in many circles. Since espionage was not his bag, it was unlikely that the security people had anything on him. However, we try to keep track of up-and-coming specialists in our own line of work, and Ernemann was coming up; in fact he could be said to have reached the top. More or less a free lance in the political field—there was no evidence that he'd ever accepted a syndicate or private contract although I had a hunch he might be willing to compromise his principles if there was enough money involved—he was supposed to be particularly good with automatic weapons. He was supposed to be, also, a pretty good woodsman and a hell of a mountain climber. His idea of relaxation, apparently, was scrambling around precipices for fun, hanging by his toenails and pitons, if I've got the right word. It's not my idea of splendid outdoors sport; I get dizzy when the terrain gets too vertical. But the point was that, contrary to what Mac had said, Ernemann was exactly the chap you *wouldn't* pick for dirty work in dark alleys. His forte was fresh-air assassination.

It was my cue. It mean that, lacking time to be fancy, Mac had been using a direct mirror code to brief me, and everything he said—everything of any importance, at least—had to be reversed before it made sense. He'd told me not to try to prove I'd been framed; that meant I was supposed to work at it. He'd ordered me to give my-

self up; that meant I was supposed to stay at liberty as
long as possible. He'd told me our relations with our opposite numbers in Mexico were terrible and contact was
forbidden; that meant I was supposed to get down there
and look up a Mexican agent at once.

What Mexican agent? Well, Mac had referred me to
the fiasco of an assignment I'd had down there involving
UFOs, which had actually been a fairly successful mission. (In case you're wondering and worrying, the You-
foes had been strictly phony.) It had been run from the
Mexican end by an impressively competent operative
named Ramón Solana-Ruiz. Apparently we were working with Ramón again, Norma was trying to make contact, and I was supposed to locate him, too, or hope that
he'd get in touch with me once I was safe in Mexico.

Finally, there was the question of the individual who,
Mac had said, objected to being referred to as a Chinaman. Well, there was only one Oriental for whom we used
that word, derogatory or not—a Peking emissary with
whom I'd had some dealings in the past. Just how he fit-
ted into the puzzle wasn't really clear—if anything was—
but Mac had used a lot of tortured verbiage to warn me
about him, so obviously he was of some significance.

Well, Mr. Soo could wait. In the meantime, the situation, as far as I could piece it together, involved two of
our people, both of whom I'd worked with before, tracking down a known professional hitman who, for some
reason, had made himself a little too unpopular in Washington. Just what he'd done to achieve this unpopularity
remained unspecified. Talking against time, on a bugged
line, Mac apparently had figured it was information I
could do without for a while. It occurred to me that we
had some things in common besides our work, Ernemann
and I. He was, according to the record, younger, blonder,
and a bit heavier than I was, and one inch shorter; but if
somebody wanted to do a spot of impersonation, and had
Ernemann and a bottle of hair dye handy, he might just

possibly get away with it in places I didn't visit frequently, like certain banks.

It was an intriguing thought, and I intended to keep it in mind, but again there were matters of more immediate importance. Apparently our two agents had suddenly found themselves in trouble with our security people, presumably for having large, unexplained sums of money in their bank accounts, like me. At least, although Mac hadn't been specific on this point, it seemed likely that the same type of frame had been used for us all. Roger, real name Jack Salter, had been arrested. Norma had made it into Mexico, perhaps because her Spanish blood and knowledge of the language—her true name was Virginia Dominguez—had given her a bit of an edge down there along the border. Or maybe she'd simply been following Ernemann's trail south and still had no idea of the situation she'd left behind.

The question was, then: where did I come in? The answer wasn't difficult. I was, after all, the unofficial troubleshooter, the patsy who usually got the job of cleaning up the baby after somebody else had dropped the diaper and lost the safety pins. Now, with hindsight, I decided that Mac could very well have sent me to the goddamned ranch so he'd have me handy out here if things went wrong. Only, some foresighted and well-heeled individual or organization, acquainted with our setup, had gone to a lot of trouble and expense to put out of action, not only the two operatives who were threatening to embarrass their hired hand Ernemann in the performance of his current chores, presumably homicidal, but also the backup man who'd undoubtedly come after them if they got into difficulties.

"You're not very chatty."

I glanced at the woman behind the wheel. "You picked me up, ma'am. It's your party. Anyway, I wanted to see if we were being followed before I got engrossed in conversation."

"Are we?"

"Apparently not."

"Oh, good. I really mustn't be seen with you. I mean, I just can't afford to be connected with. . . . Oh, damn!"

She was trying to get across a four-lane thoroughfare, one of several that have been plowed, in the name of progress, through the pleasantly cluttered old Spanish-style town I used to live in. Of course, being that kind of a driver, she couldn't move until traffic had come to a complete standstill all over the southwestern United States, or at least all parts of New Mexico visible to her.

"Oh, shut up!"

She spoke irritably, as somebody honked behind her, where cars were piling up. Then, the boulevard was deserted and we crept across.

She glanced at me apologetically. "You see, I have to be very careful. Oscar gets so angry if I get the slightest dent in any of the cars, even my own."

"Oscar?"

"My husband. He doesn't know I'm. . . . He's off on one of his Mexican fishing trips, thank Heaven, and he thinks I'm in Sedona, Arizona, visiting friends up Oak Creek Canyon. If he even dreamed I. . . . Oh, dear, it's such a mess, isn't it?"

The funny thing was, she didn't look at all the timid, breathless way she talked. She was a big girl in a smart, yellowish pants suit, a floppy-brimmed matching hat, a creamy silk blouse with a scarf at the throat, and expensive brown shoes with square heels less clumsy-looking than most these boxy days. In size, she was close to Amazonish: a gray-eyed, brown-haired, sweet-faced female nearly six feet tall and not skinny. Well, I guess it figured in a way. There are two kinds of big girls, the ones who're proud of it, and the others, who've spent their lives apologizing for it and won't quit until they're dead. Having got into the habit, they tend to apologize for everything else as well. There was something familiar about the shape of her face.

"Salter," I said.

She glanced at me quickly. "I'm Clarissa O'Hearn, Mr. Helm. Mrs. Oscar O'Hearn."

I didn't ask how she'd learned my name; it was becoming obvious. "Go to hell," I said. "You're Jack Salter's older sister. He mentioned you when we worked together some years back. A handsome fellow was needed, never mind the sexy details, and they said I didn't qualify, I can't imagine why. It hurt my feelings very badly, I can tell you. But I do remember those attractive, smiling, boyish features. . . . The funny thing was, for a tooth-paste-ad type, he turned out to be a pretty good man to have around, if you made allowances for his impulsive nature."

She said, "I'm surprised that you can see a resemblance. Everybody always said poor Clarissa, Jack certainly got all the looks in that family. I used to hate him for it when I was younger. Yes, he's my kid brother. He's in trouble; he was expecting to be arrested any minute, so he sent me to warn you."

"Some warning," I said. "You've trailed me around for three days without a word."

She looked surprised and hurt. "Oh, did you see me? I thought I was being very careful." When I made no comment, she went on: "I . . . I couldn't make up my mind. I really shouldn't risk . . . I don't dare get involved, really. I mean, you don't seem to understand. Oscar *O'Hearn.* You must have heard of. . . ."

"Oh, the department store O'Hearn," I said.

That shocked her mildly. "Oscar wouldn't like that," she said. "He's in so many other things nowadays besides O'Hearn, Incorporated. . . . But you can understand why I have to be careful, even if Jack is my brother, can't you? Actually, I was hoping to catch you at breakfast this morning, at your hotel. I'd really made up my mind to talk with you, and then I overslept a little. When I came in to see if you were still there, they were asking for you at the desk, sounding very official and nasty, so I knew if I was going to be any help at all I had to catch you. . . ."

"So you drove over to the Chevy place, knowing I was about to close the deal, and tailed me to the bank, and finally got up enough nerve to make the contact." I frowned, thinking hard. She didn't speak. I said, "Well, I'm going to need reliable transportation and that rental car I've been driving sounds like a terminal case. . . . Maybe I can pick up my new vehicle before they unravel my trail. Would you mind taking me there? But don't get too close."

She drove for a little, and asked without turning her head: "How much?"

"What?"

"How much did you find in *your* bank that wasn't supposed to be there?"

"Twenty grand," I said. "In this account. I gather there's a matching sum elsewhere. How much was planted on Roger?"

"Roger?"

"Sorry, that's Jack's code name with us, Mrs. O'Hearn. I suppose you know he works for the U.S. government."

"Yes," she said primly, "if you want to call it work. I made him tell me something about it before I agreed to help by coming here to find you, and I must say. . . . Well, before Watergate and all that stuff I'd have been absolutely horrified. Even now I find it hard to believe that my own country . . . my own brother . . . but he never told me what he was called."

"Sure," I said mildly. You get used to it. They expect protection, all the respectable citizens. If they don't want to know how it's achieved, why do they keep asking? I said, "You didn't tell me how much was planted on him."

"Oh," she said, "well, it was exactly the same amount,

Mr. Helm. Twenty thousand in his Phoenix account; and another twenty in Tucson, but he didn't have time to go there, he just checked by phone. But he took out the Phoenix money, all of it. Half he kept for expenses and the other half, well, he gave me that to give to you. He said, if anything happened, you should . . . you should find the man responsible and cram it down the bastard's throat; that is, unless you preferred to insert it into the other end of his alimentary canal." She was a little pink, looking straight ahead as she drove. "I'm giving you his exact words, Mr. Helm, as he asked me to. Personally, I think it's very stupid and . . . and childish. Thinking about petty retaliation when you're facing disgrace and imprisonment!" She hesitated, glanced at me, and asked curiously: "Did you take your money out? I mean, the part that didn't belong there?"

"Naturally," I said. "As much as I could without attracting attention. I expect to use part of it, like Roger, for necessary expenditures, but I'm sure as hell going to make the guy who framed me eat whatever's left. Civilized forbearance isn't a habit with guys like Roger and me, Mrs. O'Hearn. I'm afraid we're just natural-born, eye-for-an-eye, tooth-for-a-tooth retaliators."

It sounded good, tough and menacing. I couldn't help remembering, however, that it's difficult to stuff a guy full of hundred-dollar bills, from either end, when you haven't the faintest idea who he is.

three ••••••••••••••••••••••••••

As far as I'm concerned, what Detroit does best is the half-ton truck. I'd had one as my personal transportation when I lived out there. After my marriage broke up, and I went back to work for Mac, I made the mistake of using it on one job too many, and lost it off the side of a mountain, with a little help. That had been a two-wheel-drive pickup with a so-called camper shell over the bed that protected my gear and gave me a place to sleep if I was caught out at night. It was painted dull green and had originally cost me, as I recall, a little over two grand.

My present acquisition, with power to all four wheels, was a nine-passenger station wagon on a truck chassis, called a carryall. I don't know eight people I care to drive around with all at once, so I'd had the rear seat yanked out. The middle seat folded neatly into the floor. That left me plenty of room for a mattress and sleeping bag back there, plus quantities of hunting gear, not that it mattered now. The equipment I'd been preparing was piled in a corner of my hotel room, and I wasn't about to take the risk of trying to retrieve it under the noses of Euler's men.

The new vehicle was four times as expensive and four times as glamorous as its predecessor, with a flashy blue-and-white paint job and, so help me, flossy blue tweed upholstery. Why, with vinyl available, any sane person would want delicate cloth upholstery in a rugged boon-docks vehicle remained a mystery to me, but being short of time I'd settle for what they'd had on the lot. It looked enormous among the low, sleek passenger cars parked outside the salesroom.

"You're all set to go, Matt," said the salesman. I'd never seen him before we commenced negotiations, but he'd been giving my first name a workout from the moment he'd learned it. "I even managed to promote you a license plate on short notice; I've got a friend over in the Department of Motor Vehicles. Your registration's in the glove compartment." He patted the hood as we stopped by the husky carryall. "She's been all checked over, and you've got a full tank of gas, thirty-one gallons; it's the oversized tank, remember. And don't forget what I showed you—she's in four-wheel drive all the time. There's no messing around with the front hubs like on the old jeeps. If you really need traction, just pull that transfer-case lever into lock, low or high. But don't leave it there when you get back to dry pavement or you'll strain something." He shook my hand. "Thanks for the business, Matt, and good hunting."

I glanced at him sharply, suspecting irony, but he was obviously quite sincere. Nobody'd been at him yet. He didn't know that, instead of being the hunter, as in the original script, I was now the hunted. He really wasn't a bad guy despite the Matt-old-pal act I'd found a bit jar-ring after my months overseas where they address their customers more formally. At least he was conscien-tious and knew his business. You'd be surprised how many of them can't begin to tell you the gas tank capacities or rear end ratios of the high-priced dreamboats they're trying to peddle.

I climbed to the lofty seat—those 4WD jobs ride a bit higher than even regular trucks. I turned the key in the ignition and the big V8 up front came to life with satisfactory promptness. The salesman gave us a farewell salute as we rolled magnificently off the lot and onto the street, pausing to let a battered old Volkswagen go by, almost too small for us to bother about; but we were tolerant, we didn't squash tiny insects unnecessarily.

It had been some time since I'd sat at the wheel of a commercial vehicle, and I'd forgotten how much better the view was from up there. I could see right over most of the traffic ahead. For all its size and weight, and its stiff newness, the monster was quite responsive. I wouldn't have wanted to try cornering it with a Jag or Ferrari; but then, a sports car or any other car wouldn't last long trying to follow it across country, something I planned to keep in mind. Conspicuous and a bit unwieldy, it wasn't exactly the chariot I'd have selected to cope with the situation that now confronted me, but it did have its advantages. . . .

She was still where I'd left her: big, timid, sweet-faced Mrs. Oscar O'Hearn. It was something I wouldn't have bet on. After all, she'd completed her mission. She'd warned me. She'd handed over Roger's ten thousand bucks, making me a walking mint. There wasn't really any good reason for her to hang around except that I'd asked her to—there were some questions I thought she might be able to answer. But the Continental was still parked down the side street where I'd left it. She got out when she saw me. I'd told her what to expect, and she could hardly miss the shiny blue beast coming around the corner. I started to pull up behind the Lincoln, glancing instinctively at the rearview mirror as I slowed. In the glass, I saw a Volkswagen turning the corner behind me.

It was quite obviously the one I'd just missed as I'd left

the Chevy dealer's lot, a white bug of uncertain vintage. The front bumper had led a hard life. One fender had had a dent hammered out amateurishly and covered with paint that wasn't quite the right shade of white. I remembered my fleeting thought that Andrew Euler's people wouldn't use a Lincoln where a Volksie would do. Apparently my ESP was in fine shape. It was just my common sense that was lacking. I'd been so intrigued with my new three-ton toy that I'd neglected to take the elementary precautions.

It was too late to drive on. I'd already hit the brakes; the flash of the tail lights would have told the driver astern where I'd intended to stop even if I kept going. Anyway, there was the lady standing by the big coupe expectantly. He'd have her description and her car's fixed in his mind already; the veriest rookie couldn't overlook a striking combination like that. I pulled up behind the Lincoln.

The bug rolled past. One man. Brown hair, worn fashionably shaggy but not too long. Horn-rimmed glasses on a boyish, pug-nosed face. One of the clean-cut lads, oozing dedication and sincerity, probably with a high-class degree in something from somewhere, now saving the U.S. from treason and subversion. Not that my eyes are good enough to spot all that with one glance at a passing car, but I'd had a few encounters with security before. It's a calling that seems to draw humorless fanatics, young and old, like red syrup attracts hummingbirds.

You know that he has always been a good friend of this organization, Mac had said, speaking of Euler. Like most of the things he'd said, that statement had been exactly reversed from the truth. Actually, Andrew Euler was known to hate our guts with moralistic fervor. It was his contention that a nasty outfit like ours did not belong in the kind of nice, civilized, democratic government for which he acted as self-appointed conscience. In this connection, his attitude was much like that of Mrs. Oscar O'Hearn.

We'd looked after our own security for years, with reasonable success, but Euler was a reform-type empire builder like so many in Washington. After taking over the Bureau of Internal Security, he'd gradually established it as the nation's sole defense against those who would destroy us from within, a shocking number to hear him tell it. His doomsday approach had impressed enough legislators that he'd finally been given the right to extend his poking and prying into even the darker corners of governmental activity previously forbidden to him, like ours. What he'd learned about Mac's operation had upset him seriously. Its existence, he'd announced, was a blot on the otherwise stainless moral fabric of our nation that should be erased at once.

A field man myself, I don't keep up with all the bureaucratic infighting that goes on in that town, but reliable sources had reported to me that Euler had succeeded in getting himself slapped down hard. Mac is an old bureaucratic infighter from away back; and he's survived a lot of idealistic reformers. Since then, friend Andrew had refrained from further frontal attacks, but our routine security checkups under the new dispensation tended to be on the vindictive side. Nobody doubted that he was hoping to get something on us sooner or later and make it stick; something, for instance, like three agents with large sums of money in the bank they couldn't, or wouldn't, account for. . . .

"Some folks wait for the all-clear before they come out of their foxholes," I said as Clarissa O'Hearn came up to the truck. "Others get their heads shot off."

Her eyes widened, and she glanced in the direction the VW had taken. "You mean—"

"I'm sorry," I said. "It wasn't your fault; he'd have spotted your car even if you'd been lying on the floor. I goofed. But that's almost certainly a government snoop, maybe one of those you saw at my hotel. I figure he's been to the bank where he learned about the draft made out in my name, payable to Mr. Chevrolet. He was on his way there to ask questions when he saw me driving away and recognized me. He turned around and followed. Of course I should have spotted him behind me; I was just too damned entranced by all my pretty new knobs and levers. You can kick me if you like."

"Oh, dear," she said helplessly. "Oh, dear, what do you think he'll do? What can we do?"

"Well," I said, "as soon as he gets to a phone he'll undoubtedly report my contact with a handsome six-foot dame with a twelve-grand turnpike cruiser, Arizona license whatever-it-is. So we'd better not let him get to a phone until we've had time to think this over. I suggest a little ride in the country before he can find himself a booth and a dime. . . ."

four ....

Formerly, leaving Santa Fe southwards, you were out in coyote-and-prairie-dog country almost immediately; nowadays, the town peters out gradually through a dismal twilight zone of gas stations and drive-ins and housing developments that no self-respecting wild canine or rodent would tolerate. The desert is still out there, however; you just have to drive a little farther to find it.

Checking the mirrors—the outside ones were big truck-style jobs that gave a fine wide-screen view—I saw Clarissa coming along bravely in her royal-blue chariot, although she was undoubtedly sweating blood at the sizzling velocity of fifty-five miles per hour. Farther back, the shabby white Volkswagen was also keeping station in a commendable fashion, trying to hide itself as much as possible behind larger vehicles. It had no visible radio antenna. There was always the possiblity of a walkie-talkie instrument of some kind, but that was the kind of expensive gadgetry that I hoped Mr. Euler's underprivileged minions had to struggle along without. There was a good possibility, I decided, that I'd detached the guy from his task group—Strike Force Helm?—without anybody being aware of it but him, at least for the moment.

A few miles out of town, I swung off the four-lane highway onto a secondary road. The first time I took that road, years ago, it was a real wilderness experience; now the arroyos have all been bridged, and the thoroughfare has been graded, widened, and paved, taking all the adventure out of it. It was a nice morning for driving, however; the kind of day on which, out there, you can see farther than a citizen of the smoky East, or the smoggy West, would believe possible. There was heavy snow on the higher elevations of the twelve-thousand-foot Sangre de Cristo Mountains towering behind us; this winter the skiers had it made. There were even occasional patches of snow in the deeper shade down where we were. Elsewhere the plains were yellow-brown except for the distinct green shapes of the desert junipers, very individualistic and antisocial little trees growng well apart from each other.

I led my three-car caravan through an old mining town and up through the hills beyond and down the other side, more or less driving by the seat of my pants. The new-road construction had changed things around a bit since I was last there. I was heading for a spot in the next range of hills that I remembered. Presently I pulled off onto a ranch road and stopped to open a gate in a barbed wire fence. I got back behind the wheel to drive through it, leaving room enough behind the truck for the Continental. After getting out again and closing the gate behind us, I stopped by the coupe. The power window slid down smoothly. Clarissa's face had a worried look.

"Should we . . . I mean, this is private property, isn't it?"

Respectable people always amaze me. Her whole life as wealthy Mrs. Oscar O'Hearn might be at stake, but the lady was worrying about a spot of trespass!

I grinned. "What the hell kind of an Arizona girl are

you, Mrs. O? Remember the old Western saying: 'Signs are for people; fences are for cows.' I don't see any 'posted' signs, do you? Not that I'd let them bother me if I did, with my career and your reputation at stake."

"I'm not really an Arizona girl," she said. "I'm a transplanted Pennsylvanian."

"I know. The rich and aristocratic part of Philadelphia, no less. Your brother was always kidding about what his snooty ancestors would do if they could see him. . . . Ah, our boy almost overran us," I said, watching the road. "Now he's going to wait back in that dip where we can't see. . . . Okay. We've still got him on the string. When he starts after us again, it'll take him a little while to work the gate; that'll give us a lead. Now, please do exactly what I tell you. . . ."

In spite of the changes that had been made in the area, I'd hit the right place. The dim ranch road took us straight into the hills, dwindling into a couple of wheel-tracks running up a shallow wash that gradually got deeper and steeper until it graduated from the arroyo class and became a real little canyon. The bottom was sandy, and the road crossed and recrossed it; a nasty spot to be caught in a flash flood. Judging by the clear sky, there was no risk of that today, but long ago I'd come up here with my family—well, my wife had remarried, so it was another man's family now—looking for a pleasant, private spot for a picnic. The clouds had pulled together up ahead, thunder had started to roll, and we'd got the hell out fast, but for some reason the place had stuck in my memory all these years. . . .

The side arroyo was just where I recalled it. I cut left across the sandy canyon floor. In the mirrors, I saw Clarissa drive on up the road as instructed, in the big car that wasn't exactly made for this kind of work. Well, she didn't have much farther to go. Fortunately, this kind of work was exactly what my vehicle had been made for. When the wheels started to dig into the sand, I grabbed the big lever sticking out of the floor and dragged it into the locked position, just as the salesman had told me. It worked. With all four wheels pulling hard, we paddle-wheeled across the main canyon, found solid ground again, and crawled up into the left-hand branch until a rock wall hid us from sight.

Stopping, I took advantage of the pause to get out the adhesive tape and the plastic bags I'd picked up in the drug store, and the two ten-grand rolls of bills, original owner unknown, from my account and Roger's. Working rapidly, I taped packets of money to myself and to the car, in places I hoped weren't too obvious. By the time I was finished, I could hear the doodlebug coming. Then the sound stopped. I moved out to where I could peek around the corner of rock, wondering what was taking our shadow so long. We'd hit nothing below that should have bothered a Volkswagen.

But he was just being careful, stopping to scout ahead on foot whenever the road, such as it was, looked favorable for an ambush. I saw him stick his head out briefly; a few minutes later I heard the distinctive note of the flat-four motor again. There he came, feeling his way slowly. At the fork, where my side canyon branched off, he stopped and looked around once more. My tracks were clear in the sand—well, that's not quite true. It was obvious that something had been driven across the canyon at some time since the last water had run there and smoothed everything out, but these days people drive jeeps all over the desert, and it's hard to tell the age of wheel-tracks in soft sand. Clear, they're not.

The young BIS man frowned at the blurred tire-furrows and seemed about to investigate them further; then some sounds drifted down the canyon from above and caused him to look that way. There was a lot of back-and-forth grinding up there; obviously a car in trouble, trying to get out. He climbed back into his Volkswagen and headed that way.

When he was gone, I threw the truck into reverse and backed quickly out of there. I had no room to turn; I just kept her rolling astern through the deep sand and back onto the road. I remembered to unlock the transfer case; the salesman would have been proud of me. I'm not, as you'll gather, a four-wheel-drive expert. I used to think a good man ought to be able to get a conventional vehicle just about anywhere. The few times when a true off-road machine has really been needed in the line of duty, I've always had a trained jeep-jockey assigned to manage it for me. I'd bought this 4x4 merely to give me a nice, safe edge over the unknown hitman—as I'd thought him—in the Lincoln, in the rugged country to which I'd planned to decoy him. Well, it was a gambit that could be applied to cars other than Lincolns.

I put the truck into forward gear and headed after the Volkswagen. We had him between us now. He was in the bag.

five ....

I didn't drive right up there, of course, even though I don't have a great deal of respect for the Security boys. I picked a narrow spot well below, where the truck would block the road effectively. I set the brake and departed on foot, leaving the carryall locked behind me. If he did manage to slip by me, he'd need two keys to move it, one for the doors and one for the ignition: the newest example of the peculiar modern auto-merchandising principle that the convenience of the cash customer doesn't mean a damned thing as long as you can please the insurance companies and the Feds. Personally, I'd prefer to use just one handy key for everything and take my chance of being ripped off, but I was only the guy who'd paid for the bucket so naturally nobody'd asked me.

I made my way up there silently, keeping among the rocks. When I peeked out, he was nowhere in sight. There were no people to be seen in the little hollow ahead, just the two cars. There was the Lincoln, empty and locked, barring the road upwards, with tire-tracks showing where it had been run back and forth several times to make the appropriate stuck-in-the-sand noises. Behind it was the Volkswagen, also empty, with the door hanging open. I glanced at my watch and settled down to wait.

He'd shown promise below with his cautious approach, but he disappointed me now. He wasn't really very good. I'd been afraid he'd outlast the lady, whom I'd instructed to stay in hiding but didn't trust very far. I needn't have worried. Eleven minutes of desert silence was all he could take. Then he came sneaking out from behind a boulder and made a dash for his car. He got it going. He got it turned around although he didn't have much room; even with that short wheelbase it took a lot of backing and filling. Then he was bouncing recklessly downhill past my hiding place. What the hell he thought he was accomplishing I had no idea. I mean, he'd just run the route, hadn't he? He'd seen what kind of a single-track railroad it was. He couldn't possibly believe that I'd be considerate enough to go to a lot of trouble to park my big vehicle off to the side so he could drive away, could he?

I sighed, and shuffled back down there cautiously, taking my time, and taking no chances. You've got to be careful, dealing with idiots. They're apt to catch you by surprise by doing something so dumb you wouldn't believe a grown person could actually behave like that.

When I got down there, the Volkswagen was stopped, almost touching the truck's massive front bumper. He'd gone just as far as he could go. He was standing by his car, looking around fearfully, gun in hand. I frowned. He seemed to be overreacting to the situation. I mean, those boys are generally pretty cocky, not to say arrogant. They're used to pushing, not to being pushed. I hadn't expected him to grasp, really grasp, that the low, traitorous type he'd been tailing in a routine way had actually set a trap for him. The folks with whom his organization normally dealt didn't fight back, except perhaps with lawyers and words.

But this guy was in a pants-wetting panic. I didn't like it. He obviously knew something I didn't. He was acting as if he thought I had a very good reason to set traps for him, a reason quite apart from the fact that he was doing his duty as a good little security man. There was only one explanation for his behavior that I could think of. . . .

He whirled to face the road leading uphill. Like him, I'd heard a small clicking sound from that direction, where somebody had accidentally kicked a loose rock that had bounced against another rock. I slipped over that way, and there was my female ally sneaking down the primitive track in her fashionable pale yellow pants suit, carrying her wide-brimmed hat in her hand. I guess she'd taken it off when she hid so he wouldn't spot it among the rocks. Well, that was bright enough, but what she was doing now wasn't. She'd been told to stay put until I came for her. She gave a little gasp as I slid down beside her.

"Twenty yards more and you're dead," I said. "He's got a gun down there and he's nervous as a wet cat. Just scale your hat out there and see."

"My *hat?*" She sounded as if the sacrifice was unthinkable and I was a beast for even suggesting it.

"Okay, but get over between those rocks and cover your face with your arms. It's only in the movies that ricochets don't splatter a lot of stuff around." I waited until she was reasonably well sheltered, selected a rock about the size of a grapefruit, and rolled it down the road. He fired three times. I thought only the first two shots were intentional; at least they were the only ones that came our way, whining off the rocks and spraying splinters everywhere. The third was one he'd tried to stop but couldn't get the message in time to his over-anxious trigger finger although, realizing he'd been tricked, he'd already relaxed his aim. I lowered my arms and brushed dust out of my hair. "You see what I mean?" I asked.

Mrs. O'Hearn was upset. "What's the matter with

him?" she demanded indignantly. "He's supposed to be a . . . a kind of officer of the law, isn't he? Can he just open fire on anybody like that, without warning or anything?"

I grinned. "That's my girl. Just keep the law clearly in mind, doll. Somebody has to."

"I'm not your girl, Mr. Helm," she said stiffly, "and I'm not anybody's doll. A six-foot, hundred-and-seventy-pound doll? Don't be silly!"

Being shot at seemed to have given her some gumption, and an unexpected sense of humor. I said, "Sorry for the familiarity, ma'am. Could I respectfully request that you stay right here for a few minutes?"

"What are you going to do?"

"If he likes to shoot, let's keep him shooting, by all means. I doubt he's overburdened with ammunition; it would spoil the drape of his haberdashery. In the Volksie, perhaps, but not on him. I've never seen the routine used effectively in real life, but there's always a first time. Now stay put so I know where I have you, please."

I sneaked off to the left, since that was the side of the cars he'd been on when last seen. When I found a place from which I could cover the area, and peeked out cautiously, he was still there, although he'd moved between the vehicles for better cover. I didn't even ask myself why he hadn't taken this opportunity to slip away; I didn't have to. The answer was plain in his natty sports coat, sincere tie, sharply creased slacks, and shiny shoes. I had him trapped as completely as if I'd built an eight-foot chain-link fence around him, charged with fifty-thousand volts. He was a city boy, probably an eastern city boy. His car was his sole link with civilization. The idea of leaving it hadn't even occurred to him. What, strike out on foot and *walk* five miles to the highway? Through the *desert?*

I took out my .38 Special, aimed it at the sky, and pulled the trigger. He whirled and shot at the noise, twice, knocking chips from some nearby boulders. I stood up and laughed at him.

I'd hoped my appearance would draw a last hasty shot —that is, I hoped it was his last—but he just crouched there gripping his revolver with both hands, the way they're taught nowadays. I'm old enough to have learned one-handed, and it still looks peculiar to me. The shot I wanted didn't come.

"Drop it or use it," I shouted. "Last chance for the kewpie doll."

His face was shiny down there, although the day wasn't hot. I wondered again about the cause of his fear. It would be nice to think that I have such an awe-inspiring reputation, in Washington and elsewhere, that trained security agents turn green at the thought of confronting Horrible Helm in person. Honesty compels me to admit, however, that most of my fellow government employees have never heard of me; and those few who have mostly consider me just another of those weirdo spooks operating out of just another of those weirdo spook shops that waste the taxpayers' money playing "I Spy." Even though this guy had a little more information about our activities than most, he was taking it too big. He just had to have a guilty conscience to perspire so hard, about something that concerned me or my organization. I didn't like to think what it might be.

The range was seventy-five yards, give or take five. That's stretching a short-barreled .38 under the best circumstances possible. I wasn't a bit certain I could hit him unless I took a solid rest against something. I was willing to gamble that he couldn't hit me, even using both hands. Of course there's always the lucky shot; but you can waste your whole life worrying about the guy with the silver bullet that's meant for you.

"Any time, Lone Ranger," I called. "Fire at will."

I saw him lick his lips down there and start to shout

back, but he thought better of it. I took a step towards him, and another, picking the easiest way down the rocky hillside, sweating a little myself as I waited out the shot. . . .

"Over here."

It was a feminine voice from off to the right—my right, his left. A large yellow object came sailing through the air. The BIS man whirled and fired instinctively, and the wide-brimmed hat soared a little farther and settled to the dusty ground. I aimed high and pulled the trigger of my Smith and Wesson. Whipsawed, threatened from two sides, he swung back to shoot at me, but his hammer fell on a fired chamber, telling me what I needed to know. He dropped the revolver and raised his hands. I went over and picked up the yellow hat and brushed it off. Clarissa O'Hearn appeared where the road ducked in among the boulders, and came forward a little uncertainly.

"I told you to stay put," I said.

She said defensively, "I told you. I'm not your girl and I'm not your doll." She took the hat from my hands and examined it. "He didn't hit it."

"No."

"What are you, a hero or something?" she demanded with sudden anger. "Standing there begging him to shoot holes in you!"

She drew a long, rather shaky breath. "But what in the world is he so frightened about, Mr. Helm? I mean, you're undoubtedly a dreadful man, but you don't scare me that much, and I scare fairly easily."

We both looked at the clean-cut young government employee with the horn-rimmed glasses, standing with his hands in the air although no such order had been given. I took the girl's arm and led her that way. When we came up, he faced us bravely for a moment, then looked away.

"I think it's bad news, Mrs. O," I said.

Clarissa frowned. "What do you mean?"

"I think Roger is dead," I said. "He was arrested, you

know, just as he expected, and it's the only answer that makes any sense. I think you're looking at your brother's murderer—one of your brother's murderers."

"That's not true!" the BIS man gasped. "It isn't murder when . . . He was a government prisoner trying to. . . . It was incredible. He went absolutely ape; he grabbed a gun from his guard and started to. . . . We had no choice. He made us kill him!"

I steadied the girl as she turned sharply and pressed her face against my shoulder.

six ••••••••••••••••••••••••••••••••

Under more favorable circumstances, I'd have been more appreciative of the pleasant armful she made, more feminine and less substantial than she looked. I felt her straighten up, regaining control of herself with an effort.

"Okay?" I asked, releasing her.

"Yes," she breathed. "Yes, I'm okay. But . . ."

"What?"

"Jack didn't *do* it! It wasn't his money in those stupid bank accounts! To *kill* him . . . !" Her voice broke.

"I know," I said. I looked at the BIS character, whose arms were obviously getting tired up there, as if I cared. "What's your name?" I asked.

"Kotis," he said. "Gregory Kotis. Look, Helm . . ."

"What did he say to you, Gregory Kotis?"

"What?"

"Jack Salter," I said. It was beginning to add up, but there were still a few numbers missing. "Code name Roger. A handsome chap with theatrical inclinations and the money to indulge them. I believe he'd actually had

44

some Broadway experience before he found a different and more exciting outlet for his dramatic talents with us. But old habits die hard. Roger wouldn't have gone out without a curtain speech, if he could possibly swing it. What was it?"

Kotis licked his lips. "Salter said . . . he said we were all dead men. *Have fun,* he whispered, looking up at us, particularly Mr. Euler, *have fun as long as you last. As of now you're the walking dead. Helm will. . . ."* Kotis licked his lips once more. "That's all. Then he died."

After a moment I said, "Old Roger always did have a ghoulish sense of humor. Obviously you didn't take him seriously, or you wouldn't have ventured to tail me out of town all by yourself."

"Well, I couldn't stop to contact Mr. Euler at his hotel without losing you; and anyway, one gets hardened to melodramatic threats." Kotis tried for a bit of brave nonchalance. "Somebody's always going to get us if it's the last thing he does, and it never happens. It wasn't until . . . until I got up into this weird crack in the hills and saw the crazy way you'd set the trap. . . . Just what the hell do you think you're doing, Helm? You're a fugitive from justice. You must know you can't possibly get away with . . ."

I sighed wearily. "Mr. Kotis, the last man who told me what I couldn't get away with got a nice, sharp knife inserted into his anatomy, all the way. Don't tempt me. This trigger pulls real easy." After a little, I went on: "So you realized you weren't in a very nice spot, and those melodramatic threats came back to haunt you. Is that why you hit the panic button?"

He didn't answer that. He said, "Look, my arms are getting tired, can't I—"

"Any time," I said. "Of course, when you lower them I'll blow a hole in you as big as your fist, but go right ahead if you think it's worth it."

His arms, about to relax, became rigid once more. He said angrily, "Goddamn it, Helm, you're way out of line! We both work for the same employer—"

I stared at him, surprised. "You can't have it both ways, *amigo*. If I'm a fugitive from justice, I'm not working for anybody but me. Anyway, I wouldn't take orders from that self-righteous fanatic you work for, not for a thousand bucks a minute."

"Mr. Euler isn't . . ." He stopped that. "I didn't mean Mr. Euler. I meant the United States of America."

I regarded him for a moment, with a little more respect. I said, "I'm supposed to be a traitor, a high-priced, forty-grand Benedict Arnold. Why waste the patriot routine on me?" I shook my head. "And on the other hand, if we are working for the same employer, as you say, the same country, what the hell are *you* doing here? Why are you interfering with a government mission and shooting down trained and valuable government agents—all in the line of your patriotic duty? How do you justify that, Mr. Kotis?"

"Salter was under arrest—"

"For something any fool can see is a frame."

"We've got evidence—"

"Money in the bank? Getting money out of a bank is the hard part; any fool can put it in."

"He had ten thousand of it on him! If he was so innocent, why didn't he protest at once that it didn't belong to him, instead of drawing it out and sneaking off with it?"

"Maybe he had the strange notion that if he did protest, nobody'd believe him."

"We have the sworn statement of a witness who claims to have paid you and Salter and others for services contrary to the interest of—"

"You see?" I said. "Roger was perfectly right."

"What do you mean?"

"If he had protested that the money wasn't his, you wouldn't have believed him. You'd have taken the word of a professional turncoat and professional liar—look up the record of this guy Groening, or Gerber, or Gulick some time—against the word of a U.S. agent with a fine record who'd risked his life for his country a dozen times. Your chief is so eager to get us that on the word of a cheap fink he'll have us arrested and dragged off and shot. . . . Where?"

"What?"

"You heard me. Where was Roger taken so that you could kill him at your leisure?"

"I told you, it wasn't like that! He tried to—"

"Never mind *how* it was." His eyes told me I was on the trail of something important. "I was asking you *where* it was."

Kotis hesitated. "I'm not at liberty to tell you where," he said stiffly, at last. "And we were perfectly justified in what we did. After all, he had a gun—"

"Pretty damned sloppy work, I'd say, letting a prisoner reach a gun."

"Maybe, but if he was innocent, why did he make a break like that?"

I looked at Kotis bleakly for a moment. "Break?" I said. "What the hell gave you the idea he was making a break?"

"I was there! I saw—"

"And I'm here; and I know a lot more about guys like Roger than you do, my friend. Who do you think you're dealing with, anyway? What the hell kind of tender characters do you think take on our kind of work?"

Kotis frowned. "What are you trying to say, Helm?"

I said grimly, "I'm trying to say that you're dealing with a special kind of people, and Roger was just a little more special than most. He was one of the real go-for-broke boys. Impulsive, you might say. Great nations often find such individuals very useful, Mr. Kotis, properly supervised and controlled—these days it's hard to find folks who haven't been brainwashed to think they're supposed to live forever. We grab all of them we can get; even so, it's hard to keep a supply on hand since they are, so to speak, self-expendable. You'll have to check the psychological profile to see how Roger got that way. My guess is he'd always resented being a pretty, rich boy. Maybe he thought he had to prove that a guy could be handsome and wealthy and still be smart and tough and dangerous." I glanced at the woman beside me. "How about it, Mrs. O'Hearn?"

She had a damp handerchief clutched in her hand, and her eyes were red. She nodded. "Jack was always having to prove something, I'm afraid."

I shrugged. "Okay. Maybe he joined us to show up all those who figured he had to be a pansy because of his looks and money. Hell, I don't know. I do know that the one time I worked with him I kept clearly in mind, as always with guys like that, that I was teamed up with General George Armstrong Custer looking for his Last Stand. I didn't let him find it, but apparently you and your outfit did. That poses a question, Mr. Kotis. Roger needed to get good and sore at somebody before he'd really blow up. Like I told his sister just now, he was a natural-born retaliator; but a bunch of civil servants legally and courteously investigating a peculiar frame-up wouldn't have set him off. Just what the hell did you people do to light the fuse?"

There was again that embarrassed hesitation. Kotis said, "Why, we . . . we were just interrogating—"

I said, "Interrogating. Sure. That's all Torquemada ever did, as I recall. Although he didn't call it interrogation; he called it inquisition. Well, we'll learn the details eventually, don't think we won't, but never kid yourself for a moment that Roger was making a violent break for freedom. For one thing, it's against our ground rules in the case of a legal arrest in this country, even one based on a frame or misunderstanding. For another, if he'd really been trying to escape, being a pro he'd probably have made it. No, I figure you bastards simply annoyed him past the point of no return. . . . How many?"

"What?"

"How many?" I snapped. "How many of you did he get before you burned him?"

Kotis swallowed. "Three. And one, the guard from whom he got the gun, is totally paralyzed and slowly dying from a bullet in the head. I've never seen anything . . . just like target practice. It was horrible. He was just standing there firing deliberately, one, two, three, and they were going down like. . . . That's when Mr. Euler and I . . . everybody was charging in there shooting . . . and then, when we went over, your man was lying there grinning like a wolf. A satisfied wolf. And he told us we were all dead. And died." The BIS man shivered slightly. "I've been trying to understand . . . Salter couldn't possibly have hoped . . . he wasn't even trying to run."

"There's nothing very difficult to understand," I said. "You took an innocent man arrested on phony evidence, a man trained to kill, and then you were stupid enough to push him around enough to make him even madder than he already was. What the hell did you expect? At that point, all he wanted was to take a reasonable number of you sons of bitches to hell with him, which is exactly what he did. Now, wherever he is, he's having a lot of fun hoping that, after the fancy buildup he gave me with his dying breath, you'll put me in a spot where I'll have to make a few more gory additions to his death list. . . . Thanks a lot, Roger, old pal!" I grimaced. "Oh, hell, put your arms down before they fall off. How about answering a few questions? I won't ask you anything top secret, I promise."

Kotis lowered his arms and flexed them gratefully. "What do you want to know?"

"I presume, in interrogating Roger, you asked what he was doing in this part of the country besides putting illicit money into the bank. What was his answer?"

"He said he was on the trail of a man, a dangerous man."

"The name?"

"I can't remember. Actually, under the circumstances, we didn't take his story too seriously. . . . Oh, all right, it was German, like an old camera. . . . Voightlander? No, Ernemann. That's it, Ernemann. According to your agent Salter, this Ernemann was on a deadly mission in Mexico and it was Salter's duty to intercept and dispose of him."

"And the target of this deadly mission?"

"According to Salter, the proposed victim was a Mexican general with political ambitions—he's been in the papers from time to time, I think—named Hernando Díaz." Kotis laughed shortly. "Well, that's what Salter said. Not a very likely story, is it: an American agent assigned to protect a Mexican army officer in Mexico. They don't love us so much down there that they come asking us for that kind of help in internal matters. Obviously, it was just Salter's convenient excuse. . . . After all, we caught him just as he was about to slip across the border south of Yuma."

"Sure. Great work. Did he tell you anything interesting about his associates on the job?"

"Oh, yes. He told us about you—the backup man, he called you—and the girl he was working with; only she escaped into Mexico before we could pick her up. Not very reticent, your friend Salter."

"We're permitted to use any information we have any way we think may earn us a break, except in special cases, when we're given a death capsule with orders to take it if capture is imminent. Don't sneer at a dead man when you don't know the rules he was playing under."

Kotis swallowed. "Sorry."

"What about the girl? You say she got away from you?"

"Yes, she made it over the border before we could arrest her. Code name Norma, Salter told us. Real name

Virginia Dominguez. Miss Dominguez has twenty thousand dollars to explain. Of course, Groening had already told us about her; we just asked Salter as a check on the information we had."

I said, "Norma had better get in touch with Women's Lib. Here we male chauvinist pigs wind up with forty grand apiece and she's stuck with a lousy twenty. I suppose that, just like Roger and me, she was stupid enough to put it into the bank under her own name."

"The description of the depositor—"

"How many pretty, dark-haired, dark-eyed little girls are there in this part of the world who'd run an errand like that for a twenty-dollar bill and ask no questions afterwards?" I shook my head. "Hell, if you close your eyes and throw three rocks across the Plaza in Santa Fe, at least one is bound to hit a sexy brunette named Salazar or Montoya or Martinez or Dominguez. Just like you can hardly pitch a pebble across a California surfing beach without bruising a tanned and handsome fellow who looks pretty much like Roger—well, like Roger did."

"Helm, you're being ridiculous!" Kotis said. "You can't really expect to convince us that somebody not only spent a total of a hundred thousand dollars just to frame you and your two associates, but also went to the trouble of finding two men and a woman to impersonate you."

Well, it was the reaction I'd expected, wasn't it? I said patiently: "Have you read a description of our friend Ernemann? Six feet three, blue eyes. Does that put you in mind of anybody you've encountered recently, Mr. Kotis?" I shook my head again. "Never mind. Just stick it on the back burner and let it simmer. In the meantime, I'm going off to one side to hold a consultation with the lady. Subject: the future, if any, of Mr. Gregory Kotis." I reached down to pick up the empty revolver he'd dropped. "Do you keep any refills around for this toy?"

He hesitated. "There's a box in the glove compartment of my car."

I reached in and got it. He made no effort to take advantage of the distraction. Straightening up, I said, "You've got a choice. You can stand right here or you can run like hell. I'll just point out that I'm a top-notch tracker and a red-hot *pistolero*. Also, I know this country like the palm of my hand; I used to live out here. But if you think you can beat those odds, you're welcome to try. . . . This way, ma'am."

As we walked away, I reloaded the two firearms from Kotis's supply. His weapon was a Colt .38 Special, the same caliber as the Smith and Wesson I carried, but with the cylinder drilled for six holes instead of five. Clarissa, walking beside me, was brushing the last traces of dust from her yellow hat and putting it back on. I realized that the floppy hat, like the rest of her stylish pants outfit, was actually constructed of corduroy. Back when I was a kid, this was considered very low-class material, on a par with poor-folks' denim; but any day now I expect to see them making glamorous evening gowns of burlap and canvas—maybe they already have. Kotis, I noted, was standing motionless where he'd been left.

Clarissa looked that way, and back to me. "You seem to have impressed him. But I wouldn't say modesty was your greatest virtue, Mr. Helm."

I grinned. "Hell, I've only been up in these particular hills once before in my life, I'm a pretty fair rifle shot but I'm only mediocre with a pistol, and any Apache off the reservation can track rings around me. But I didn't have to tell him that, did I?" I stopped grinning. "Here."

She drew back from Kotis's freshly loaded revolver as I held it out. "What . . . what's that for?"

"If you want him, he's yours. I owe you that much for being careless and leading him to you. Anyway, Roger was just kind of an associate of mine; he was your brother."

"You mean . . . you mean you want me to *kill* that man?"

I said, "Frankly, I'd rather keep him alive, Mrs. O. I have a use for him alive; that's why I went to all this trouble to capture him. But alive he can talk. That doesn't bother me. He knows nothing about me the rest of his gang doesn't know or can't find out. It's different with you. Unless they've done some fast investigating of Roger's family, they don't even know you exist. Certainly they don't know you're anywhere in this neighborhood, and they can't prove you've had anything to do with me. This boy does and can. He can put the finger on you. Give it some thought, Mrs. O. I may be able to keep you clear if Kotis is silenced. If he remains alive he'll eventually blow the whistle on you. There's a way of stopping that. Right here."

She was staring at me in the incredulous way they do when you start applying logic to life and death, and it comes up death. She licked her lips.

"You must know I can't possibly . . . I can't even believe we're standing here talking like this. Why, it would be *murder*. No!"

I said, "I got you into this. Well, all the way in. Now I'm showing you a way out. Don't blame me, later, because you didn't take it."

She studied me for a moment. A faint smile touched her lips. "Mr. Helm, I think you're pulling my leg: the ruthless secret agent shocking the innocent little girl, and you certainly did shock me. But it was a put-on, wasn't it, Mr. Helm?"

After a little, I grinned. "Well, kind of. But the main idea was to show you that the only reasonably foolproof way out of this for you is a way you can't take. I'm sorry, but that's the way it is. If you're ready to accept that, let's go."

She hesitated. "Go where?"

"Ernemann was heading for Mexico; he has a date with a Mexican general, Kotis tells us, even if the general may not know it yet. Roger was about to cross the border when they picked him up. Norma is known to have slipped into Mexico. Obviously, that's where the action is, so that's where I'm going. And since your tender heart condemns us to turning Kotis loose eventually to shoot off his mouth about you, just about your only way of working your way clear of this now is to stick with me and help me find out just who's doing what to whom. Okay?"

She drew a long breath. "Okay, Mr. Helm."

We walked back to the neatly dressed young man waiting by the cars. Eight hours later we were closing in on Douglas, Arizona.

seven ....

You can't miss Douglas. Nobody can miss Douglas. They mine copper down there along the border, and the high, white smoke plumes from the smelters are visible long before you come through the last mountain range, which doesn't amount to much, and see the town ahead.

We'd left the Lincoln and the Volkswagen standing where they'd stopped back in the New Mexico hills, much to Clarissa's distress. There would have been certain advantages to taking her car—mainly that it wasn't known and my truck was, or would be as soon as Euler's boys did their homework—but I didn't think it would make a great deal of difference. Even before Andrew Euler took it over, the Bureau of Internal Security hadn't been noted for cooperating with local authorities. Jealous as Euler was of his prerogatives, I didn't think I had to worry much about state policemen or all-points bulletins. He'd want to catch me himself; he'd inform the local law only when he was ready to try me for treason, or bury me.

As for the carryall, Mexico is a country where a rugged vehicle often comes in handy. Anyway, I'd just paid big money for the beast; I wasn't going to leave it behind to be impounded as evidence or whatever. My experience has been that whenever the government, God bless it, gets hold of your property, for any reason, you play hell getting it back.

The border-crossing closest to Santa Fe is the big El Paso-Juarez installation due south, with the little one at nearby Columbus, New Mexico, not much if any farther. The trouble with these two escape hatches, from my point of view, was very simple: you can't get there from there. They both put you on Mexican highways leading south or east. To get west, without first driving halfway down to Mexico City, you've got to pick up their Highway #2, which originates in Agua Prieta, just opposite Douglas. I had to keep in mind that Roger had been apprehended in Yuma, in the far southwestern corner of Arizona. Even farther west, Norma had crossed from California into Mexico by way of Tijuana—about as far as you can go in that direction without getting your feet wet. Everything indicated that they'd planned a rendezvous out in Baja California, and if I was going to make contact with the girl, I'd better make a large try at getting out there and figuring out where.

In the meantime, with the town of Douglas visible ahead, I turned off onto an unpaved side road, stopped the carryall, and got out and walked around it. I yanked open the rear door on Clarissa's side, pulled a handsome fringed blanket—we'd swiped it from the Lincoln—off the shapeless object lying there, and hauled Kotis out to where he could sit up with a little help. He was taped like a mummy.

"Hang on tight," I said. "This won't be fun." I freed a corner of the tape and removed his gag with a quick jerk. "Okay?"

He worked his mouth around in his face until his lips regained some function. "Where are we?" he asked at last.

"The metropolis under the smoke is Douglas, Arizona."

"Arizona? That means we've crossed a state line. You know what the penalty for kidnaping is, Helm!"

I grinned. "Sure. It's roughly the same as that for homicide, so I've got nothing to lose by shooting you dead, right?" I shook my head sadly. "Anyway, what's this nonsense about kidnaping? You're a prisoner in Federal custody. . . . Aw, shucks, I forgot to arrest you, didn't I? Gregory Kotis, by the powers vested in me by the United States of America, I hereby place you under arrest as accessory to the murder of a U.S. officer, one John Salter, engaged in the performance of his official duties."

"But you can't do that!" Kotis said, aghast. "I mean, you people aren't empowered . . . our authority supersedes . . ."

I gave him my mean grin again. "If we don't watch out, we'll sound like a couple of kids saying my dad can lick your dad. Empowered or not, I've seen very few authorities superseding a .38 Special. Don't make any mistakes, Kotis. Your authority means absolutely nothing to me. The same goes for Mr. Euler's authority. As far as I'm concerned, you Security people are nothing but dangerous nuisances. My job at the moment is to take over a certain assignment from the man you arrested and shot down. In other words, I have work to do and I'm going to do it. And if you die in the process, or even Euler himself, it's just too goddamned bad. You boys should have been smart and stayed out of my hair. It's not my fault if people commit suicide, is it?"

Kotis said angrily, "Now, listen, you arrogant—"

"Easy!" I snapped. "Take it just a little easy, friend. Don't make it too hard for me to keep you alive. I'm trying to make allowances, remembering that I have information you don't have if you're a sincere and honest man. That, of course, remains to be proved."

"What information?" he demanded.

I said, "I'm reasonably certain that neither Roger nor Norma took money under the table to sell out their country. I know damned well I didn't. That makes you, Mr. Kotis, part of a gang of government thugs employing your special powers, and phony evidence, to railroad three innocent people, one of whom you've already killed. Of course, you may simply be misguided, letting yourselves be used by somebody wanting us out of the way who's rigged a fancy scheme based on your chief's well-known hatred for my chief. On the other hand, I'm not overlooking the possibility that you folks just got tired of waiting for us to make a security slip that would let you clobber us, and set up the frame yourselves—"

"You can't believe that!" Kotis gasped. "I didn't . . . Mr. Euler wouldn't . . . !"

"Maybe," I said. "But let me make a little bet with you, Kotis. I'll bet ten bucks, cash, that the guard in the hospital with a bullet in his skull was not shot with his own gun."

Kotis frowned. "I . . . I don't understand. What are you driving at, Helm?"

"Think about it," I said. "Sneak a look at the ballistics report some time. And after you've worked things out, I think you'll understand why I'm not about to let myself be arrested on the basis of your idiotic evidence. Roger submitted trustingly, as the rules require, knowing he was innocent and figuring he'd be able to prove it; now he's dead. Anybody who thinks I'm going to forget that little object lesson has got his head screwed on backwards. If you boys want me, you're going to have to take me. Roger cost you three or four men. I'm better than he was, if I do say so myself. I'm older, uglier, smarter, tougher, and meaner. The price is high, friend Kotis. How much blood are you willing to spill to get me? How much is your boss willing to spill?"

Kotis started to speak and stopped, obviously convinced that he was dealing with a homicidal madman with delusions of grandeur. Fine. I had him in the proper mood. He wouldn't pull any grandstand plays under the impression that I was a normal human being who'd be normally reluctant to blow out a fellow-agent's brains.

I said, "Now that we've got that clear, let's get the stickum off your wrists and ankles, after which you can flip up that back seat for me and get up front beside the lady. . . . Okay, Mrs. O'Hearn, you drive. It's an automatic shift. Works just like a Lincoln. Stop at the first filling station inside town. As I recall, there used to be a public phone . . ."

The phone was still there. It was Ma Bell's newfangled equipment, the kind that just protects the instrument and to hell with the customer—I couldn't help wondering again what had happened to the old-fashioned notion that you're supposed to be nice to the folks who purchase your goods or services. I stood in front of it with Clarissa close on one side. Kotis was on the other, covered by my Smith and Wesson, hidden between our bodies. I wanted them both to hear what was said, as much as possible, to save me from having to go over it again.

A familiar male voice spoke in the phone: "Yes, operator, I'll accept the charges."

"Eric here, sir," I said.

"Where are you, Matt?" So the emergency line was still bugged. Good.

It was time for me to do my rabid-dog routine once more, this time for a larger audience. I made my voice sharp and nasty. "What's with this everlasting concern for geography, sir?" I demanded. "Never mind where the hell I am. Have you got your red pencil handy?"

There was a little silence. "Report," said Mac's voice softly at last.

"Scratch Agent Roger, the Adonis of the undercover services," I said harshly. "After arresting him in Yuma, our nonviolent colleague Euler's gentle disciples apparently took him somewhere and worked him over until he got mad enough to grab a gun; then they mowed him down. Nice, friendly, peace-loving chaps. I am happy to report that Roger did some mowing of his own. Three for-sures and one probable. Do you still advise me to surrender like a good boy, sir?"

There was another silence, broken at last: "It is a . . . very regrettable incident. You may be sure it will be investigated very thoroughly. However, I am unable to change your instructions. You are still under orders to turn yourself in."

I said, "Some orders! Hell, if you were any kind of chief for this monkey circus, you'd be out there finding out who rigged phony evidence against three of your people, instead of washing your hands of them and telling them to surrender to a BIS murder squad."

"Matt, I'll hear no more such talk from an employee of this agency!" he said sharply. "I'm sure you must be misinformed. Mr. Euler undoubtedly has a good explanation of the unfortunate occurrence. Let's be honest, we both know that Roger, while a good agent, was sometimes . . . well, a bit impulsive and headstrong."

I said, "Sure. And we both know that I'm a bit headstrong and impulsive, too, sometimes. Like right now. I've heard your instructions, sir. Now I'm giving you mine, for a switch. Can you reach Euler?"

For all I knew, the head of the Bureau of Internal Security was listening as we talked; certainly he'd be hearing tapes of the conversation shortly. However, I was not supposed to be aware of this, and Mac went along with the gag.

"I can try, although he tends to be rather elusive. But—"

"You'd better try hard, sir. Because if you don't, there's going to be one hell of a big, bloody, smoking mess on the Mexican border for you and Mr. Euler to explain to all the nice folks in Washington, D.C., and Mexido, D.F., I figure that, after missing me in Santa Fe, he had the border closed up tight. Well, I'm going through anyway."

"Matt, be reasonable. You can't—"

"Roger was reasonable, at least to start with, and he's dead," I said. "I'm not about to be reasonable, sir; it's too goddamned fatal. I'm going through. I'm putting that big new heap of mine in gear and I'm crossing the line. They can't miss it. It's shiny blue and white, it stands almost six feet high, and the gross vehicle weight is a bit over three tons. They'll see me coming. I've got one of Euler's boys with me, named Gregory Kotis. He's right beside me now with a gun in his navel, which will soon be somewhat enlarged if he doesn't . . . Ah, that's better."

"Matt, do you really think you can blackmail Mr. Euler into letting you—"

"Kotis is one of the people who helped shoot down Roger. I'd as soon blast him to hell as not," I said. "Roger was a good man. And I've also got another hostage, sir. A Mrs. O'Hearn who happened to be handy. I picked her because she was driving a big, important-looking car, and I lucked out. It turns out that her husband, Mr. Oscar O'Hearn, owns all of Arizona that doesn't belong to the jackrabbits and the Pima Indians. You can have lots and lots of fun, you and Euler, explaining to this influential gent how his wife got killed because of an intramural squabble between two government agencies. I'm sure he'll be fascinated."

"Matt, you've taken leave of your senses—"

I said, "Very good, sir! Oh, very good indeed! You obviously have the situation clearly in mind: you've got a senseless maniac heading for the border with a powerful truck, two hostages, a couple of loaded guns, plenty of spare ammo, and a very itchy trigger finger. Your own private senseless maniac, sir. Call me Frankenstein, Junior."

"I believe," he said carefully, "that Frankenstein was the creator, not the monster, Matt."

"Well, you're the creator, all right, and you know better than anybody what kind of a monster you made. You've used it often enough for your own purposes. Now I'm using me for my purposes, sir. I've got two bullets earmarked, one for each hostage. The rest are for any hostile targets that present themselves—Americans, Mexicans, Apaches, or Tarahumara headhunters, I don't give a damn. If they try to stop me, they'll need a couple of front loaders to shovel up the bodies afterwards. Nobody's making a sitting target of me the way they did Roger. They can get me, but they'll have to take me moving, and I'll be moving fast. *And* shooting back. Pass the word, sir."

He took another five-count before he spoke. "Exactly what do you want, Matt?"

"No interference," I said. "I go through clean, not a fingermark on me, or I die right there with lots of company. Hell, it's as good a place as any to say goodbye, a damn sight better than Euler's private agent-assassination preserve, wherever that may be. Tell him he can let me pass; or he can have a one-man massacre he'll never forget."

"Where?"

I hesitated; but even if the call hadn't been traced by this time, which was unlikely, Euler could pretty well figure out where I had to go.

"It's the crossing between Douglas, Arizona, and Agua Prieta, Sonora."

"Very well. I'll try to convince Mr. Euler that you mean business, much as I disapprove, but I can't promise that I'll be able to persuade him to let you through."

You had to hand it to the guy. Even in a time of stress, he could correct me about Frankenstein, and remember the nice distinction, almost forgotten nowadays, between convince and persuade.

I said grimly, "If not, you'd better warn the local undertakers to brace themselves for a rush of business. Tell Euler I hit the gate in one hour, with or without fireworks. His choice."

eight ·····························

We stood there for a moment after I'd hung up. The filling station attendant had, I saw, finished topping up the oversized tank of the carryall. I had gas for three or four hundred miles—but the first mile into Mexico was the tough one.

"I didn't know I was a hostage," Clarissa said, looking at me reproachfully.

"If you're coming along," I said, "there's no reason I shouldn't make use of your presence, is there? Of course, you're free to bail out if you like. As you heard, it could get rough. Make up your mind." I turned to Kotis. "Stick very close while I go over and sign the charge ticket. . . . Mrs. O, if you're coming, you can get back behind the wheel and start her up."

Clarissa hesitated. Then her shoulders moved in a kind of helpless shrug under the yellow corduroy of her nicely tailored jacket, and she walked away towards the truck, a big, good-looking young woman. She'd have made a truly striking figure if she'd stood up straight instead of slouching in an effort to make herself look smaller. Her motives in sticking with me weren't quite clear to me, but then, I didn't think they were quite clear to her, either. I shepherded Kotis over to where the attendant waited by the charge machine; two minutes later we were driving away.

The stalling that followed was bad; it always is. Riding around covering Kotis from the back seat and checking my watch frequently, I tried to put myself into Euler's mind, but I didn't have much success since I didn't really know the man. If he was as tough as Mac, I didn't have much longer to live: Mac plays the hostage game with nobody and for nobody, and the standing orders by which we operate read accordingly. I didn't take a great deal of pride in what I was doing. It's always a lousy business. I could excuse myself with the fact that one of my hostages was actually a volunteer of sorts, while the other deserved no consideration from me after what he'd helped do to one of my colleagues. Nevertheless, it was still a crummy way to put pressure on anybody, even Andrew Euler, and I wouldn't have done it if I'd had a choice.

I gave a final glance at my watch. "Sixty-five minutes. That's long enough. One way or another he should be ready for us. . . . Take a right at the next corner," I said to Clarissa. "Any trouble, and you hit the floor, remember? And you, Mr. Kotis, behave yourself and don't bother to tell me I'm crazy and can't get away with it. You'd better hope I get away with it."

"I'll be good," the BIS man said. "But of course you are insane. You know that, don't you?"

It was fairly courageous of him, and his voice was steady. He wasn't much of an agent, by our standards, but he wasn't a total loss.

I grinned. "We all have our little insanities, Kotis. Maybe one day you'll find some of your own. . . . Mrs. O, please take us down through that underpass. Now right at the corner up ahead. Okay, we're on the glide path, two blocks from touchdown. . . . I surely do hope your boss values your services highly, Mr. Kotis, and can't bear the thought of losing them."

The man in front of me cleared his throat. "Why don't you ask him? There he is."

We were approaching the border gate. A man stood there watching us come. I drew a long breath and cocked the revolver I held.

"Don't!" said Kotis sharply, hearing the click. "Look, he's alone. He's telling you it's all clear."

The gate drew closer. There was, as Kotis had said, nobody in sight except the single, waiting figure. I didn't kid myself it was my cleverness that had cleared the trail, if it was really cleared. The guy who was running interference for me here was Roger. Those kamikaze lads can really shake you when they decide to make that final, screaming dive into the flaming muzzles of the guns. With Roger's example fresh in his mind, Euler had apparently decided he couldn't afford to meet another of Mac's wild men head-on. Well, it was the reaction I'd been working for, wasn't it?

I gave the guy full credit nevertheless. It required something in the way of guts to handle it personally. After all, I might, being a hopelessly erratic and unpredictable nut by my own telephone testimony, have decided to pay off for Roger while I had the chance and to hell with the consequences. But Euler stood there calmly, watching us approach.

"Stop me beside him," I said to Clarissa.

"Matt, I . . . I think I'm going to be sick."

"No, you aren't," I said. "You're a big, brave girl and you just dote on thrills and excitement."

"What's my size got to do with being scared?" she asked resentfully, but her voice was steadier. Beside her, Kotis sat stiffly erect on the front seat, silent and motionless.

The truck rolled to a halt beside the waiting man.

There were no visible signs of an ambush. Off to the left, in the northbound lane, a dusty station wagon full of kids and luggage had just come to a stop, obviously homeward bound after a nice family tour of Mexico. The U.S. Customs man was going into his act, quite normally. He didn't even bother to look our way. Maybe he'd been told not to. Actually they don't give a damn what you take out of the country—that's the Mexicans' worry.

There was, of course, the possibility that a delayed-action trap had been set for me—I remembered the furor caused a while back when some overeager border or Army personnel had yanked back into the U.S. a deserter who'd already made it across the line into Canada. It could be that Euler was going to allay my suspicions, waiting until I'd stepped over the critical international boundary and relaxed, thinking myself safe, and then he would lower the boom somehow. . . .

I looked over into Agua Prieta beyond the gate. To the left was nothing but a row of shabby little shops, *cantinas*, and offices selling Mexican insurance to incoming U.S. tourists. To the right was the Customs and Immigration Building, with its small parking area. A truck full of Mexican soldiers was standing there in plain sight. A non-com of some kind—I don't have the ranks and ratings straight down there—lounged by the tailgate, chatting with a civilian wearing a dark suit and big sunglasses. As I watched, the civilian took off his glasses and started polishing them with a large, immaculate white handkerchief, after first shaking it out with an elegant snap of his wrist. He turned to look my way casually.

I let my pent up breath escape, and eased my grip on the revolver a bit. There were going to be no over-eager infringements upon Mexican sovereignty. I knew the man. I could guess that the white handkerchief, the traditional flag of truce, was a signal to me that all was safe south of the border and the situation was firmly under control, being in the capable hands of *Señor* Ramón Solana-Ruiz, who'd once saved my life and was now standing by to perform an encore, if necessary. Of course, I'd done a few things for him, too.

Euler was waiting. I rolled down the window between us.

"You're ten minutes late," he said. "You said one hour."

"I wanted to give you plenty of time to make your arrangements, or unmake them," I said.

"You can congratulate yourself on the success of your terrorist tactics, Mr. Helm. There will be no interference." His voice was bitter and contemptuous.

He was a compact man of medium height, in a brown business suit, a pink shirt, and a dark red tie, dark enough that it would have looked reasonably conservative in other surroundings, but I couldn't figure the shirt. Some folks just think pink is pretty, I guess, but somehow the color scheme wasn't one I'd have expected him to select from what little I knew about him. Well, if my only mistake here concerned Euler's taste in shirts, I could live with it.

He had wiry, wavy, dark hair that was turning pepper-and-salt gray. His sideburns were almost white, giving him a distinguished, elder-statesman look. His face was squarish and deeply seamed without any suggestion that the crevasses were derived from exposure to the weather; these were indoors creases. His eyes were wrong. They were brown eyes, and they showed a hint of uncertainty that was as out of character—the character I'd constructed for him—as the pink shirt. The hallmark of the dedicated crusader is absolute assurance. It never occurs to him that he might be mistaken about anything. This man had obviously had his fundamental beliefs shaken quite recently—I could guess when. When he spoke, however, there was no uncertainty in his voice.

"You're an evil man, Helm," he said. "The world cannot afford people like you and your associates any longer.

Certainly, this country can no longer be responsible for activities like yours, regardless of what methods our enemies may use. We cannot win by descending to their level."

"Right on, Mr. Euler," I said. "Next time I see my friend Jack Salter, code name Roger, I'll tell him how you feel about homicide as an instrument of national policy. I'm sure he'll be impressed."

The wrongness in Euler's eyes deepened, and now there was a slight angry tremor in his voice when he spoke: "The man was a . . . a mad wolf! We were not expecting . . . He forced us to kill him in self-defense."

I grinned cheerfully. "As one mad wolf to another, congratulations, sir. You're catching on. It's always self-defense. Didn't you know?"

He drew a long breath, and brought his voice under control. "You're a traitor, Helm. We have proof. If you ever step on U.S. soil again, we'll be waiting."

"Sure," I said. "Well, if there's nothing else, I'll say good-bye. Your boy will be turned loose as soon as we're in the clear. Obviously, you're worried sick about him, the way you keep pestering me with questions about his welfare."

Euler threw an odd, startled look towards the man in the front seat, as if he'd forgotten all about Gregory Kotis. He looked beyond to the figure behind the wheel.

"And the lady?" he asked.

With no guns or roadblocks in sight, and Solana-Ruiz waiting pointedly with his miniature army just across the international line, I no longer had to rely on my hostages, real or phony. It was just as well to set the record straight so nobody made any desperate efforts to rescue a kidnaped millionairess.

"Ask the lady," I said. "Go ahead, tell him, Mrs. O'Hearn."

She hesitated, and spoke quite clearly: "The man you arrested on trumped-up charges and shot to death was my brother, Mr. Euler. I'm not really a hostage, I'm here of my own free will. And I think I'll continue to ride along with Mr. Helm. At least he's not hypocritical about his violence."

A strong emotion showed in Euler's shifty brown eyes for a moment, and it wasn't just anger at the way he'd been misled about her status. Then a battered pickup with Sonora plates pulled up behind us. After a moment, the driver tapped his horn impatiently.

"*Hasta la vista,* Mr. Euler," I said. "Mrs. O'Hearn, we're blocking traffic. Drive ahead, tell the Mexican official at the gate we're stopping at Customs, and take us over there. That building to the right. Park beside the military vehicle."

There was still a moment of suspense as we pulled away; then we were in Mexico. In the parking area, Clarissa stopped the carryall and slumped weakly in her seat.

"Oh, God, I'm limp and dripping as a dish rag," she said. "If that's the way you earn your living, you can have it."

I said, "You probably didn't like caviar on the first try, either. Okay, Kotis, take it real easy. You don't want to die after the war's all over—"

"That is not necessary now, *amigo.*"

Ramón Solana-Ruiz had come up behind me as I backed cautiously out of the truck with my hand on the gun in my pocket.

He said, "You do not need him now. You can send him home."

There were things to be said, like thanks, but they were better said without one of Euler's men listening. I said, "Okay, out you go, Kotis." I urged him around the carryall, and stopped him. "Just a moment and you'll be cleared for takeoff. I want to make you an apology first, and give you a warning."

He turned to look at me, surprised. "An apology?"

I said carefully, "I don't like this hostage racket. Even though I've got no reason to be considerate of your feelings, I'm sorry I had to do it, and I'm sorry you had to be. on the receiving end. That's the apology. Okay?"

He studied me for a moment, frowning, and did not answer. At last he said, "And the warning?"

"A lot of things got said along the way, some significant, some not," I said. "Maybe you'll dismiss them all as part of the general lunacy of the situation. That's your privilege. But maybe you'll wake up in the night some time and start thinking about what you were told. If so, and particularly if you decide to do something about it, watch your back. It might not be a bad idea anyway. That's my professional advice, no charge. Okay, on your way."

He hesitated, wanting to ask questions; then he turned quickly and walked diagonally across the wide street to where Euler waited just beyond the international boundary. I saw them shake hands. Euler clapped Kotis on the shoulder in a friendly fashion. They moved off together.

I went back to where Ramón was talking animatedly to Clarissa O'Hearn. Well, he'd never been backwards about approaching an attractive woman; few Latins are.

nine ·····································

I shook Ramón's hand. "That's another one I owe
you," I said. "It was a pretty sight, you and your soldier-
boys and your hanky. Remind me to buy you a *cerveza*
some time. But how the hell did you know where to
come?"

"Your chief and I worked it out," Ramón said "After
talking with you this morning, he got in touch with me
through elaborate and secret channels—I understand
there is some difficulty with your security people." He
grinned. "Your politics seem to be almost as complicated
as ours, friend Matthew. There is always one politician
grasping for power at the expense of another, is there
not? Anyway, he told me you were replacing the man we
were expecting, Salter, who had been detained, and that
you might require help at the border. Agua Prieta seemed
the most likely crossing for you to use. It was arranged
that if later information indicated you were crossing elsewhere, your chief would let me know. He did not, so here
I am." He glanced towards Clarissa. "The lady tells me
that she is Salter's sister, and that her brother has been

shot trying to escape. I thought we Mexicans had a monopoly on the *ley-de-fuga* technique of disposing of awkward prisoners. Perhaps we should charge your Mr. Euler royalties. In any case, the political situation you are leaving behind seems to be fairly serious."

"Yes, but it's not your concern, or mine either, right now," I said. "Let Mac worry about what happens north of the border, for the time being. Our business is here in Mexico. Do you have any word on this guy Ernemann? And can you tell me how to get in touch with our agent Norma—Virginia Dominguez?"

He shook his head. "At the moment, I am afraid the answer is no to both questions. I may have more information in the morning."

"Did Mac have any message for me he hadn't wanted to try to transmit over a bugged phone?"

"Again, no. He said he thought you understood what was required with respect to *Señor* Ernemann, and I could tell you anything else you needed to know." Ramón glanced at his watch. "Unfortunately, at the moment I must go and thank a certain officer for the loan of his soldiers—it pays to be punctilious when dealing with the army—and also check with some of my informants. Meanwhile, I suggest you drive on to Caborca; that is about a hundred kilometers west of the road junction at Santa Ana. Do not hurry, particularly after sunset; remember that our roads are not made for fast driving in the dark. Accommodations will be held for you at the Motel Del Camino, no matter how late you arrive. I will see you there in the morning and we will talk."

"Sure," I said. "If you're in touch with Mac in the meantime, let him know I made it all right, thanks to you." I grinned. "Oh, and please offer him my apologies for any disrespect I may have shown him during our last telephone conversation. It was necessary for dramatic effect."

"Of course." Ramón hesitated, threw a glance towards

Clarissa, and said: "I mean no slight against the unfortunate Mr. Salter, whom I met only once, when I say it is a pleasure to be working with you again, Matthew. How do you say: it is like old times?"

It was nice of him; but as we drove away I hoped it wouldn't be too much like old times, which I recalled had been pretty hairy old times upon occasion. We left the dirt streets of Agua Prieta and picked up speed on the paved highway, heading west. Presently I realized that Clarissa hadn't spoken since we'd left the border. When I glanced at her, I saw that she was watching me oddly.

"Something wrong?" I asked.

She said, with a kind of indignant rush: "Matthew Helm, do you mean to tell me that all that threatening talk—all that menacing stuff about piles of dead bodies and buckets of blood—was just *playacting?* Do you mean to say you were just *bluffing?*"

"I don't mean to say any such thing," I said. "What makes you think so?"

"You asked Mr. Solana-Ruiz to apologize to your boss because you'd been rude to him. You said it was for . . . for dramatic effect."

"Well, sure," I said. She'd played her part well; she deserved an explanation. "Look, Mrs. O, I had two problems. Remember that the telephone line was tapped. First of all, I had to conduct the conversation in such a way as not to get my chief into trouble. I couldn't give the impression that he was in any way an accessory to my treacherous and violent behavior. He had to be the loyal, sensible employer trying to reason with an insulting, disloyal employee who'd flipped his lid, right? We couldn't afford to give Euler ammunition to use against him. To that extent I suppose you could say we were both playacting."

She hesitated. "Then he doesn't believe that Jack or that girl or you took money for the reasons everybody says? It must be nice to work for somebody who has that much faith in you."

"Faith in us?" I shrugged. "Or faith in himself. I mean, he picked us, didn't he? My second problem was to make absolutely certain that Euler knew I wasn't bluffing. But the trouble with fanatic humanitarians like Euler is they've got a thing about death; they figure anybody who claims to be ready to die, for anything, has got to be either bluffing or nuts. Otherwise Euler would have thought I didn't mean it and a lot of people would have got shot. Okay?"

We had dinner in the Mexican mining town of Cananea, which is visible just as far as Douglas, for the same smoky reasons. It was dark by the time we came out of the little restaurant, with sunset just a dim red memory over the mountains to the west, through which we still had to drive. Four hours later, with Clarissa asleep on the rear seat, we reached the Motel Del Camino in Caborca. I yawned, slid down from the high seat, and made my way inside to register. The reservation was for one room with two beds in the name of *Señor* and *Señora* Matthew Helm; and Ramón had undoubtedly grinned wickedly as he phoned it in. Well, it could have been worse; he could have specified a double bed.

I took the key, drove to the door of the unit, and got out to open it; then I opened the rear door of the truck. It had been a hard day, and Mrs. Oscar O'Hearn was sleeping so soundly she didn't really wake up when I eased her out of the vehicle, walked her into the motel room, and set her down on the near bed. When I got back from retrieving her purse and the rolled-up jacket she'd been using as a pillow, and locking up the truck, she was curled up on top of the covers like a large, tired baby.

It was a neat moral problem. She'd hate me in the morning if I let her spend the night in her clothes since she had no others. On the other hand, she'd hate me in the morning if I presumed to undress her. Since I couldn't win, I took the path of least resistance and just pulled off her shoes and covered her up the way she was. Then I peeled down to my underwear and fell into the other bed; and I hate to admit it—it plays hell with my *macho* image —but the fact that an attractive adult woman was sleeping less than six feet away didn't interfere with my rest one little bit. I'd had a hard day, too.

The next thing I knew, there was daylight at the windows and Ramón was knocking at the door.

ten ....

He was sitting at a window table when I came into the motel dining room, a handsome, dark-faced man with smooth, black hair. He was wearing a sharp, dark suit, the cut of which reminded me of Europe, a white silk shirt—or what passes for silk these days—and a gray silk tie. They don't go in for sports clothes much down there when they're on business.

I sat down facing him and said, "Thanks for the loan of the razor."

"*De nada,*" he said. "It is yours. A small token of friendship, shall we say? Where is, er, Mrs. Helm?"

"You bastard," I said, grinning.

He laughed and shrugged. "I was making it easy for you, *amigo*. She is a handsome lady. What are we men for but to help each other in such matters?"

"Thanks a lot," I said, "but at the moment I'm more concerned about other matters you may be able to help me with that don't concern my sex life. Like the guy I'm supposed to be after down here. And the girl agent who's supposed to help me track him down. A little information

77

about the military gent he's been hired to hit wouldn't hurt; and I'd even condescend to listen to the name or names of the person or persons who hired him. And finally, you might tell me why an agent of the Mexican government is allowing an agent of the U.S. government to do his job for him, to wit, protecting a high-ranking Mexican officer from assassination."

It was a little sudden and a little rough for Mexico, where you can spend half your life working around politely to the subject in which you're really interested. I saw Ramón's eyes narrow; then he laughed.

"You do get right down to business, Yankee fashion, Matthew."

"Well, I'd like to get a few things discussed before the lady makes her appearance. Not that I don't trust her, or anything, but she is, after all, just along for the ride."

"Yes, that is something I think we should talk about, also," Ramón said. He signaled the waitress to take my order. When the girl had gone, he said, "But I will answer your questions first, to the best of my ability. To start with, there has been no sign of Ernemann. He was last reported in the United States. Your chief informed me that he was seen in Washington, D.C., and later in your home town of Santa Fe, New Mexico. I cannot tell you his purpose in visiting those places."

"You don't have to," I said. "He was putting money into bank accounts that didn't belong to him. Go on."

"After Santa Fe, he seems to have disappeared. There is no report of his having crossed the border into Mexico, but it is a long border and we do not have the incentive to patrol it carefully that you do. The big smuggling goes the other way. He will surface eventually, of course. When he does you will be notified at once." Ramón paused as if expecting a comment; when I made none, he went on: "Next, I can still tell you nothing about your female agent. She was given a telephone number to call when she reached Mexico; she has not called it. It is my understanding that she speaks fluent Spanish. Let us keep in mind that a Spanish-speaking Virginia Dominguez is going to attract little attention in this Spanish-speaking country if she chooses to remain inconspicuous." He pronounced the name *Veerheenya.*

"The question is, why should she choose?" I said. "Why hasn't she checked in according to instructions? Apparently she got out of the U.S. by way of Tijuana before Euler could grab her—maybe even before she knew anybody wanted to grab her. Roger got a warning to me by way of his sister, but we don't know that he managed to get through to Norma. In other words, she may not have been on her guard. That leaves a possibility that the BIS boys got their hands on her somehow and brought her back. Strange things happen in border towns like Tijuana, and unlike some people, she didn't have the Mexican army standing by to cover her getaway."

It wasn't the most diplomatic suggestion to make to a Mexican official—that a U.S. security team might have invaded Mexican territory for kidnaping purposes—but Ramón merely shrugged.

"I suppose it is a possibility; but it is not too important, is it, *amigo?* We do not need this girl. I can supply any men and women we require." When I didn't reply to this sensible, if cold-blooded analysis of the Norma situation, he went on: "As for General Hernando Díaz he is a fairly controversial figure with wide political interests, currently stationed in Baja California. We do not know who has hired his assassination. There are several potential candidates, wealthy men whose interests conflict with those of Díaz."

"But you're sure Ernemann is coming here and Díaz is his target?"

"That seems to be confirmed, both by our sources and those of your chief in Washington. And to deal with your final question, which I admit is somewhat embarrassing, I should tell you that we are having serious problems of unrest in the mountains of the mainland. I cannot go into details, the subject is classified, but I can say that one thing we do not need is the assassination of a prominent political and military figure, even in far-off Baja. A hint of antiestablishment violence elsewhere would give much encouragement to the mainland *insurgentes*. On the other hand, as I have said, there are those who do not like the general very much and would not mind seeing him dead, whether or not they have actually done anything about it. These people are influential, too. We would rather not antagonize them if we can help it."

I grinned. "What you're saying is that you'd be real happy not to have to take sides publicly, pro or con Díaz."

"Precisely." He looked pleased that I understood. "Of course, we cannot permit murder, but it was a great relief to us when we first heard these rumors about Ernemann and started investigating, to discover that someone else was interested in him also. Your agent Salter was recognized. I got in touch with your chief. It was agreed that you Americans should have the honor of disposing of *Señor* Ernemann, since you wanted him so badly. We would merely supply information and assistance, discreetly."

"Very neat," I said.

There was a question I wanted to ask: why did we want Ernemann so badly? Of course, it could simply be a routine vermin hunt—when people make themselves too objectionable, in a violent political way, it's our job to take them out. However, that's generally a one-man operation, and there are generally American interests involved. I still had no idea why Mac considered this touch important enough to assign to it two agents and a backup man. I didn't ask, however; it's never advisable to confess to too much ignorance, particularly in a foreign country. It wouldn't be the first time I'd gone after a guy without knowing why. If my conscience bothered me, I could always soothe it with the thought that, on the record, Mr. Ernemann was a gent who wouldn't really be missed, and I was, after all, promoting good international relations by saving the life of a Mexican general.

I said, "You seemed to have some reservations about my traveling companion."

He hesitated. "Let us say that there are some interesting things about this lady that I did not quite realize on our first meeting. You know who she is, of course."

"I think I know," I said. "Tell me what you know."

"I am told she is the sister of an American agent, now dead. But she is also the wife of a certain Mr. Oscar O'Hearn, is that correct?"

"So she says. I haven't seen the marriage license, so I can't vouch for the legality of the union, but it says Clarissa Salter O'Hearn on her car registration." I frowned, watching him. "Wait a minute! You're not going to tell me that the Arizona department store tycoon is also involved in this mess—"

Ramón said, "It so happens, friend Matthew, that Mr. Oscar Francis O'Hearn is a very good friend—lately a constant fishing companion—of General Hernando Díaz. As a matter of fact they are together here in Mexico at this moment. The general is on leave and they are staying at Bahia de los Angeles on the western shore of the Sea of Cortez or, if you prefer, the Gulf of California."

"Fishing?" I asked.

Ramón smiled thinly. "Well, you know how some anglers are, *amigo*. They have been doing considerable drinking, also, and in the evenings they have, from time to time, enjoyed the company of some attractive *señoritas* supplied by General Díaz. Since it is my duty to see that his life is preserved, it distresses me to have to say that I do not think the general is a very nice man. I am afraid that *Señor* O'Hearn is not a nice man, either. In fact I think he is what you would call an Ugly American."

I said, "You've got it wrong, Ramón. In the book, the

ugly American was the good guy, the crude, craggy gent who was willing to get his hands dirty to help the native people. The handsome American, the striped-pants smoothie, was the bad guy."

After I'd said it, I decided I sounded a bit like Mac, stuffily correcting me about Frankenstein, but Ramón just grinned.

"Perhaps I should read the book. In the meantime, Díaz and O'Hearn are in Bahia de los Angeles complaining loudly about the fishing; it has not been very satisfactory this year so far north in the Gulf. They have been discussing the advisability of flying south to Mulege— O'Hearn has his private plane and pilot along—or maybe farther south to Loreto, or even clear down to Cabo San Lucas where the marlin are said to be running well."

"In other words," I said, "if Ernemann has any local intelligence system at all working for him, and he's bound to have, he shouldn't have much trouble zeroing in on his conspicuous and loudmouthed target whenever he's ready. It would be nice if you had some idea where the hell this hired gun is hiding and when we can expect him."

Ramón said, rather stiffly: "We are working as hard as we can, Matthew. He has just dropped out of sight, temporarily, I am sure. When we learn something, you will be informed at once."

"Sure," I said, "but that may be too late for your precious, boozing, wenching General Díaz. In the absence of any information, I think our best bet—our only bet, in fact—is to cover the general and wait for Ernemann to come to us. Fortunately, I know a little about saltwater fishing; and I suppose you can scrounge me up enough tackle so I can hang around playing angler without arousing anybody's suspicions."

"It can be arranged." Ramón's voice was still remote and formal; they insult easily and deeply down there. "Is there anything else you require?"

"Yes, a weapon," I said. "Ernemann's a chopper freak —I use the term the good old-fashioned Al Capone way which did *not* refer to helicopters. Any kind of automatic artillery is supposed to turn him on, if I remember the dossier right. I'd better not try to tackle him with just a .38 Special."

"I may be able to provide a submachine gun of some kind. Of course, you will have to keep it well hidden; such weapons are highly illegal in this country."

"Or any country." I shook my head. "No. I try never to play another man's game. Let him have his squirt-guns. I'll take a scope-sighted hunting rifle and the proper legal permits. Let's make it a .270 if you can find one. It's a bit old-fashioned, but I've got a tender shoulder at the moment. The old .270 doesn't kick and bellow like the newfangled Magnums, but it'll reach out just as far and hit almost as hard. Tell your armorer a 4X scope is big enough, and I want the fast 130-grain load, not the heavy 150s. I'm not hunting grizzly bear." I frowned thoughtfully. "To go back a bit, what the hell is O'Hearn trying to promote with this general of yours, anyway? Maybe Díaz supplies the girls; but you say it's O'Hearn's plane, and something tells me the bills go on the expense account of O'Hearn, Inc., or one of its subsidiaries. At least that's the way it usually works when rich guys like O'Hearn start palling around with the military, or vice versa. You said Díaz had wide political interests. Could some of them be O'Hearn interests?"

Ramón didn't speak at once. At last he said, "I am sorry, *amigo*. The man is an officer in the service of my country. I do not think I had better answer that question."

I looked at him. "I guess you just answered it. And warned me about Mrs. O'Hearn. It does make one wonder, doesn't it, when the conniving millionaire's handsome young wife stumbles into the case from a totally unexpected direction. The question is, is the lady playing her husband's game, whatever it is, or does she have some fish of her own in the skillet? Or is she, after all, just an innocent girl accidentally involved in dark international intrigues because she was nice enough to run an errand for her brother?"

Ramón said, "You know better than I do how eager she was to accompany you."

"Well, I thought it was my idea at the start," I said. "But I did offer her an out at the border and she didn't take it. Okay, I'll keep my eyes open. Right now the lady in question is, presumably, just taking a shower and worrying about the crease, or lack of it, in her pants."

Ramón laughed, relaxing. "If they did not insist on wearing male trousers, they would not be confronted by these terrible masculine problems, would they?"

I grinned. "A sexist after my own heart! Let's you and me set up a new country, Ramón—there's plenty of real estate in this part of the world nobody'd miss—a country in which the girls dress like girls and the boys like boys. It would be nice to be able to tell the difference at a glance, like in the good old days, wouldn't . . . What's the matter?"

His face had hardened abruptly. His eyes had narrowed, studying me coldly across the table. When he spoke, his voice was harsh.

"What have you heard?"

"Heard?" I frowned, and spoke very carefully: "I made a joke, Ramón. Maybe it wasn't a very good joke, but—"

He drew a long breath. "I am sorry, *amigo*. I thought—"

"What?"

He hesitated, and said, "There are some things I am not allowed to tell you; things of greater importance than the financial affairs of a certain general. Please do not ask. . . . Ah, there is *Señora* O'Hearn."

We got up as Clarissa approached, and after discussing

our itinerary briefly we didn't talk about much except the
fact that you can't get fresh orange juice in restaurants in
Texas or Florida where they grow the fruit, or in any but
the fanciest establishments in Los Angeles or New York;
but in a remote roadside motel in obscure Caborca, Sonora, Mexico, they serve you delicious, fresh-squeezed
juice as a matter of course. . . .

eleven ••••••••••••••••••••••••••••••

From Caborca, the highway swings back up close to the border and follows it for a couple of hundred miles and some change. It passes just north of the Gran Desierto at the head of the Gulf of California—a real, sandy, Sahara-type desert, not just the ordinary southwestern cactus-and-greasewood plains. It crosses the Colorado River on a toll bridge (eight pesos) and a little farther west it bypasses most of the city of Mexicali if you're sharp enough to catch the proper turns. Then it climbs out of the lowlands and up into the mountainous base of the Baja California peninsula by an endless series of switchbacks that'll make you bless your power steering if you've got it (I had). Finally, it runs straight west to Tijuana, but we didn't stay with it quite that far. At the little town of Tecate, still up in the high country, we took the southwest cutoff that lowered us by easy stages to the sizable city of Ensenada, on the Pacific sixty miles down the coast.

In Ensenada, we went shopping. Respectably equipped with luggage at last, we checked into the Bahia Hotel, which I remembered from a previous visit in the line of business. It looked a little older and tireder than when I'd last seen it, but then, who doesn't?

"So we're Mr. and Mrs. Helm again," said Clarissa quietly as the door closed behind the bellboy. "Oscar isn't going to have much trouble finding grounds for divorce, is he?"

There was hostility in her voice; she didn't like me very much at the moment. As a matter of fact, she'd hardly spoken to me since we'd left Caborca, and she'd made it clear that her silence was intentional. Maybe she guessed that Ramón and I had talked about her in her absence, and that the talk hadn't been wholly favorable.

"Does Oscar want a divorce?" I asked. "Why?"

"Well, I'm not exactly poor, you know," she said. "There was a time when Oscar was in a bind and needed money, so he married the girl. He doesn't need it any longer, and matrimony's a bit of a drag. So now he'd like a divorce if he can get it on his own terms—profitable terms. Of course, I have a lot of dirty ammunition I can fire back at him. . . . That's really none of your business, is it, Mr. Helm? If we're going to have dinner, I'd better change; I look slightly grubby after two days in this outfit." She stopped, watching me, and said: "Matt?"

"What?"

"Last night, when you . . . when you put me to bed, did you want . . ." She stopped, leaving the sentence trailing.

"Want what?" I asked, deliberately obtuse.

"Me?"

I regarded her for a moment. A couple of hectic days had, as she'd suggested, kind of blurred the fashionable, crisp, immaculate, rich-lady-in-a-Lincoln image. Now she was just a big, well-built girl in comfortably sloppy corduroy with a smudged hat crammed carelessly onto her touseled brown hair. I liked her better that way, but I reminded myself that my likes and dislikes were not really very relevant to the situation.

I said severely, "Mrs. O'Hearn, I am an honorable man and I never lust after other men's wives, at least not when I'm dead on my feet."

She asked, "Are you dead on your feet now?"

There was a funny little silence. Through the windows I could see cars driving by on a boulevard that hadn't existed the last time I'd stayed here. Then there had been nothing on the oceanside but vacant real estate and docks and water. Progress had overtaken and surrounded the Bahia Hotel.

I said, "You don't look like a compulsive nympho, Mrs. O." Carefully, so as not to startle her, I stepped forward and kissed her. Her lips were cold and unresponsive. It wasn't much of a kiss. I said, "You don't act like a compulsive nympho."

"Damn you!" she whispered. "Of course I'm not a nympho, I . . . I'm just one step removed from. . . ." She stopped. After a moment she said sharply, "Oh, this is ridiculous! My brother has been shot to death. We're both fugitives from justice, if you want to call it justice. All kinds of scary international things are going on—and here we stand talking about my lousy sex life."

"Is it?" I asked.

"What?"

"Your sex life? Is it lousy?"

"What sex life?" she asked grimly. "Why talk about something that doesn't exist? Oh, Oscar did his stuff on our wedding night like a dutiful bridegroom—well, more like a mad moose, but never mind that. What I was about to say a moment ago was that, far from being a nymphomaniac, I'm just one step removed from total virginity. That was the one step. But I guess my loving husband didn't like the sample, because he's never come back for seconds. Right now he's probably getting drunk in some fancy fishing camp with a bosomy Mexican tart on his lap."

"That's the dirty ammunition you'll fire back at him if he tries to divorce you on his terms?"

"Yes, of course," she said. "I know all about his so-called fishing trips accompanied by his gorgeous tame fly-boy—there's another beautiful character for you, simply lovely—and that uniformed pimp who calls himself a Mexican general." She drew a deep, ragged breath. "But you can see how . . . how it might shake a girl's faith in her sexual attractiveness, particularly when she's always been kind of awkward and oversized. And then, when *you* casually tossed a blanket over the large body beautiful and calmly climbed into the next bed and went to sleep. . . ." She stood up, did some quick, feminine things to her hair, and buttoned up her jacket. "You can just put up with me the way I am. All I ask is nourishment. . . ."

twelve ••••••••••••••••••••••••••

It was a long, low, rustic room with a bar at the near end and a dance floor and orchestra stand in the middle. Fortunately, we were early enough that no music was being produced. I wanted to talk, and you can't expect to carry on any significant conversations with a Mexican band playing. I couldn't help remembering that the last time I'd eaten here I'd also had an attractive female companion involved in some peculiar international intrigue. . . .

Clarissa reached across the table and patted my hand. "It must be terrible," she said. "What was she like?"

"What?" I asked. "Who?"

She laughed. "You were thinking about another woman, weren't you? Another woman who had dinner with you right here in this room—and since I reminded you of her, the circumstances were probably somewhat similar. And I was thinking it must be terrible for a man to be forever pursued by demanding females insisting on sharing his bed. You have my deepest sympathy, Mr. Helm."

"My goodness," I said. "It's practically a virgin, it says, but it gets just as jealous as a real woman."

She stopped smiling abruptly. "That wasn't very nice," she murmured. "Why are you trying to make me angry?"

I said, "It's standard operating procedure. Ply them with liquor and needle them and see if they can stick to their cover stories."

"Is it standard operating procedure to tell them about it?" she asked curiously.

I shrugged. "If I get you drunk enough and sore enough you'll give yourself away whether you've been warned or not. If you've got something to give away."

"Well, I haven't," she said. "What do you suspect me of? What was Ramón telling you about me this morning? I wondered why. . . . He was friendly enough when we first met."

"He's always friendly to pretty ladies until he has reason to behave otherwise. But then he studied all the information he had about you and came to the conclusion that you're probably a very sinister and dangerous individual. . . ." I paused, watching her across the table. "Mrs. O, do you know what your husband is *really* doing down here in Baja under the cover of his alcoholic, amorous, and piscatorial exploits?"

There was a little silence. It had been kind of a bluff, and when she drained her glass abruptly I knew I had won. I signaled the waiter for another round of Margaritas.

"Oh, I see," she said slowly. "Your Mexican friend thinks I'm working with Oscar on. . . . You mean the Sanctuary Corporation, don't you?"

I said, "To be perfectly frank, my trusted Mexican colleague was quite cagy about just what the hell he did mean. Well, I don't suppose I'd volunteer a lot of secret headquarters information if he came up to operate with me in the U.S. Tell me about the Sanctuary Corporation. What is it, one of the subsidiaries of O'Hearn, Inc.?"

"Oh, no!" Clarissa sounded shocked. "No, it's much bigger than . . . You could say that Oscar is a wholly-owned subsidiary of the Sanctuary Corporation." She paused, and went on, rather daringly for her: "What I mean is, when they say pee, he scrambles for the nearest rest room."

"Go on," I said. "You're getting more fascinating by the minute."

"It's kind of weird, really," she said. "It's a bunch of international-type people that . . . Well, I guess they got the idea from something that was supposed to be tried in the Bahamas. One of the islands was supposed to be persuaded to secede peacefully and, as an independent nation, become a blissful refuge for harassed millionaires, or something. At least that was the way the rumors ran."

"I heard something about that," I said.

"Oscar was very interested and so were several other people he knew, but when he investigated on their behalf he found it wasn't a very satisfactory proposition for some reason. Or maybe he and his friends just decided they could do better on their own, closer to home—well, his home—where he already had good contacts, civilian and military, particularly military. By this time, quite a group had got together on the thing, some of them international operators big enough to use O'Hearn, Inc. for petty cash. They'd kind of taken over, and strangely enough Oscar didn't mind; in fact, he was proud to be associated with such important men. And the whole approach had changed; they were no longer thinking in terms of peaceful democratic persuasion. There's a strong revolutionary tradition south of the border. They figured that one more little military coup down there wouldn't upset the international applecart to the point where any large country, like the U.S., would feel obliged to intervene. . . . What are you laughing at?"

"Sorry," I said. "I was just remembering that I said

something playful to Ramón about starting a new country where men were men and women, women. I wondered why he didn't think it was a bit funny. . . . What have they got in mind, Baja?"

"Southern Baja California, yes. They are going to call it the Republic of Cortez. They feel that, as long as it's kept a strictly internal matter, nobody but the Mexicans will care much who governs the dismal tail end of a barren peninsula sticking a thousand miles down into the Pacific. Actually, of course, it's a very pleasant and picturesque area, but most people don't know that."

"The Sanctuary Corporation," I said thoughtfully.

"They think the world is going to hell," she said, "and they want a place to hide that's all their own, where they can make their own kind of rules for their own kind of people. Of course that comes later. Initially, it'll be a native uprising led, of course, by that great democratic leader of his people, General Hernando Díaz."

"It doesn't sound very practical to me," I said. "Even if they do have a tame general in their pocket and he has a few troops who'll obey him, they can't really believe they can take over part of Mexico and hold it indefinitely by military force."

"Not *just* military force, Matt," she said. "For one thing, Mexico has some internal problems—Baja isn't the only trouble spot. The army is quite busy up in the Sierra Madres, over on the mainland. For another, these are powerful people, rich people. It's going to be a native uprising, to be sure, but there'll be plenty of help from high-priced mercenaries—the kind of roving specialists at war who pop up at all such parties if good salaries are being paid. There'll be all the munitions anybody could want; the ships are already at sea. . . ."

"You're still talking military force," I said. "I've seen one or two of these shoestring revolutions, and I know a few people in Mexico. I don't think General Díaz, his malcontents and his mercenaries will get any farther than those boys did at the Bay of Pigs, and they had the backing of a fairly powerful corporation, if you recall."

"You're not allowing for all the factors," Clarissa said patiently. "Militarily speaking, you may be right, but you're forgetting Oscar's powerful financial friends. When the politicians in Mexico City try to pull themselves together to crush this traitor general and his upstart Republic of Cortez, they'll find nothing will work. Supplies won't be delivered, communications won't communicate, trucks won't roll, trains won't move, ships won't sail. . . . Don't think it can't happen. Among them, these men and the international conglomerates they control can pretty well strangle a small country's industries if they work together, and they're together on this."

"Mexico isn't so damn small," I said. "But I see it's a plausible enough notion that a bunch of fat industrialists impressed with their own power might think they could get away with it, and I guess they could do considerable damage before they were stopped. But there's one weak link. If they really want to make this look like a homegrown revolution, they've got to have that Mexican general. If somebody takes out Hernando Díaz, they're done, unless they're willing to reveal themselves as latter-day pirates taking over a piece of foreign real estate by naked force; and that's a precedent I doubt the U.S. would stand for so close to home, no matter how gun-shy we may be after Vietnam." I paused. Clarissa didn't speak. I said, "Is that why you hired this man Ernemann and sent him down here?"

It didn't jolt her a bit. "You and your shock tactics! Matt, you're cute," she said, laughing. "Why in the world would I care whether that country down there is called *Baja California Sur* or *El Republico de Cortez*? If you're thinking I'd go that far just to spite my husband . . ."

"Something like that," I said. "I keep getting the impression it's not a very happy marriage; I don't know why."

"Well, it isn't," she admitted frankly. "I was a stupid little girl—well, big girl—and I was flattered by the attentions of the powerful and successful man who obviously, I thought, wasn't a bit influenced by my money, unlike all the others who gritted their teeth and put on their unconvincing Romeo acts. . . . But being a disillusioned bride is one thing, and hiring a professional gunman is something else, Matt. Does your friend Solana-Ruiz think this killer is working for me?"

"Ramón didn't say so, but I wouldn't be surprised if the thought had crossed his mind." I hesitated, and probed in another direction. "It could be that you're public-spirited enough to disapprove of this project very strongly, particularly since your husband is undoubtedly using some of your money—"

Clarissa shook her head quickly, smiling. "I'm afraid you've got the wrong girl, Mr. Helm. Oh, I disapprove, and actually I wouldn't mind a bit if General Hernando Díaz fell down dead, if only I got to see Oscar's face when he heard about it. He's put a lot of work into this thing, and I think he hopes to be a very big wheel down there after they ease out the native revolutionaries and put themselves into power. But even if I knew where to rent a trained killer, which I don't, I wouldn't go that far just to get a few laughs at my husband's expense. . . ." She shook her head again, ruefully. "As for saving the poor, downtrodden peasants, well, I'm sorry but I'm just not the concerned type, Matt. Frankly, I'm getting a little tired of forever worrying about who oppresses whom; I'm certainly not going to murder people, or hire them murdered, to stop it."

After a good many years in the business, you get a feeling for when people are telling the truth and when they're lying. It isn't infallible, of course, but my instinct told me the girl was not lying, at least not very much.

My curiosity had a question to ask. "Just how did you manage to learn so much about this operation, Mrs. O?"

"I'm stupid and harmless," she said calmly. "It's just like having a big dumb heifer around the house, Oscar says, and I guess he believes it. At least he doesn't take many precautions to keep me from finding things out."

There was no bitterness in her placid voice, but I didn't take that too seriously. She might be telling the truth at the moment, but I reminded myself that she wasn't the most consistent personality I'd ever met. She'd acted terrified of driving a car across a pretty safe boulevard, but had then very neatly distracted a dangerously nervous armed man at exactly the right instant. She'd started out talking as if she were terrified of her husband; now she was discussing him with casual contempt. I had a feeling I was watching a very inhibited lady breaking free of a lot of old restraints and getting a new act together, but I couldn't quite figure out what the act was supposed to be.

I said, "Now tell me about the gorgeous flyboy."

That got more of a reaction than any of the rough stuff I'd hit her with. Suddenly pale again, she toyed with the empty glass from her latest Margarita and didn't speak for several seconds.

"It's . . . a rather painful subject, Matt. I'd rather not talk about Phil, if it's all the same to you."

"It isn't," I said. "Phil what?"

She looked up angrily. "You're really a very rude and demanding. . . ." Then she sighed. "Oh, all right. Philip Krakowski. Can you imagine me falling for a man named Krakowski? Well, I suppose Polish girls do it all the time, and I'm just being nasty and prejudiced. Actually, he's a very good pilot and a very beautiful hunk of man. Ask Phil, he'll tell you all about it . . . No, I'm being unfair; I can't help it. He's not really vain about his skill or his looks. He's just very, very confident. I gather he has reason to be. Both in the air and . . . and in bed."

I didn't say anything. The waiter brought another round of Margaritas. Clarissa picked up hers, stared at it in a hostile way, and attacked it as if destroying a dangerous enemy.

"It was . . . it was a very simple and sordid little plan," she said without looking at me. "I told you, Oscar wanted a divorce on his own terms. Not very difficult to arrange, really, if you have a shy and inexperienced wife and a handsome and experienced pilot who doesn't mind, for a substantial bonus, doing a little extra work quite unrelated to aviation. He was . . . very sweet, very considerate, very handsome, and very sympathetic about my hard lot as Oscar's wife. It almost worked. Only, before the critical bedroom scene, before any bedroom scene at all could take place, they got overconfident and careless and made the mistake of discussing me rather crudely in front of an open window."

"Tough," I said. "Or, maybe, lucky."

She drew a long, ragged breath. "Damn it, Matt, I loved the creep!" she whispered. Then, in normal tones, she said, "Now you know all about Phil Krakowski. Now let's find something more pleasant to talk about, like vultures and hyenas and cute little crawling maggots. . . ."

Actually, over dinner, we discussed the possibility of tomorrow, getting a look at the great gray whales at Scammon's Lagoon down the coast.

thirteen ••••••••••••••••••••••••

We could still hear the pounding drums and blaring horns as we stopped at the door of our room, in the wing of the hotel away from the dining room. The musicians had arrived, and pianissimo is unheard of in Mexico. I opened the door and Clarissa moved past me. There was some faint daylight left outside the windows, but the drawn curtains reduced the room illumination to a striped, shadowy twilight. I followed her inside and pulled the door shut behind me; then she was in my arms.

It seemed as natural as if, as some people do, we'd driven down to Ensenada for the purpose; and maybe in a way we had. After a little, she freed herself breathlessly, stepped back, and helped me unfasten her jacket and blouse. I slipped the garments, together, off her shoulders and arms, and dropped them onto a nearby chair.

I said, looking at her in the dusk, "My God, I haven't met one of those contraptions in years. I didn't know they still used them."

Clarissa laughed softly. "I'm just an old-fashioned, brassiere-wearing girl, Mr. Helm," she murmured. "An intoxicated, old-fashioned, brassiere-wearing girl. Go on, before I sober up and lose my nerve. It unhooks behind."

"Ah, it all comes back to me," I said, reaching around her. "I used to be pretty good with brassieres, if I do say so myself."

We disposed of the garment in question. Somewhat alcoholic and a bit impatient, I wasn't very good with the zip-up-the-front slacks but with a little help I figured out the combination and we took care of pants and panties. Somewhere along the line she'd shed her shoes, becoming a slightly smaller girl in the process, just about right for a man my height. We kissed again, at considerable length. There was something pleasantly illicit about, fully dressed, holding a substantial naked lady in my arms. I patted her lightly in the appropriate place.

"Go find us a bed, any bed," I said. "I'll be with you in a minute. . . ."

Some time later, a lot later, she stirred and pulled a sheet and blanket over us.

"Okay, Mrs. O?" I asked.

"Okay, Mr. H." She moved a little closer. "Well, I knew, in spite of Oscar, there had to be something nice about it, the fuss everybody makes," she whispered, and went to sleep.

I didn't sleep right away. I lay beside her watching the last faint stripes of daylight fade from the ceiling and listening to the distant beat of the Mexican band. . . .

In the morning, having gone to bed early, we woke early. There was a funny constraint between us as dressing, we tried to adjust to our new relationship without discussing it directly. We compared hangovers very brightly instead, and decided that the rumors that the ethnic Mexican booze contained in last night's Margaritas left no aftereffects had undoubtedly been invented by a clever PR man for the tequila-mescal-pulqe industry. A crisis occurred when it turned out that the tough and practical traveling clothes she'd bought herself yesterday were ridiculously small.

"But I got the largest they had!" she protested, almost tearfully.

"Six-foot Mexican ladies aren't common," I said, and grinned at the way she looked, standing in the bathroom doorway in the pants that wouldn't zip and the shirt that wouldn't button. I picked up the pile of garments she'd worn previously and tossed it to her. "Here."

"Mat, I can't go around forever looking like a tramp who's been sleeping in the woodshed!"

"Why the hell not?" I asked. "This is Baja California, the last frontier. We're driving a rugged, dusty, half-ton truck. If it'll make you feel better, I'll pass up shaving and we'll be wilderness tramps together. In any case, we can't hang around here waiting for the stores to open; we've got a pretty long drive today."

She made a face at me, and disappeared into the bathroom. Fifteen minutes later we were leaving Ensenada without breakfast, since the hotel dining room wouldn't open until seven. A hundred and twenty-five miles south, at Bahia San Quintin, we found the first of the new El Presidente hotels sponsored by the Mexican government to assure tourists of reasonable accommodations along the newly paved Baja highway. It was an elaborate establishment, and we caught up on the meal we'd missed in a handsome restaurant facing the beach.

"It's a little late to ask," Clarissa said presently as the waiter filled her coffee cup for the third time, "but where are we actually going?"

"I told you," I said. "We're going to Guerrero Negro to see the whales."

"You said something about whales but you never mentioned any Guerrero Negro," she said. "That means Black Warrior, doesn't it?"

"Something like that," I said. "But we did talk about

Scammon's Lagoon, remember? The little town of Guerrero Negro is close by, I'm told. Actually, we aren't going
to either the lagoon or the town, although if you really
yearn to throw peanuts to the whales maybe we can sneak
off this evening for a little. But in the morning, we've got
a fancy secret-agent-type rendezvous down a little desert
road I hope I can find, where we'll take delivery of some
equipment without being observed. . . ."

The new Baja highway is not a major engineering miracle. The valleys and gorges barring the way are not
spanned by soaring bridges; the road just crawls and wig-
gles down one side and up the other. The hills and ridges
have not been blasted apart by high explosives and
shoved aside by giant machines; mostly the road just
climbs over them. And where there's a desert wash or arroyo where water runs hard during the rare rains, there's
seldom a culvert; there are just two sets of stakes marked
in meters to indicate the edges of the ford when flooded,
and whether or not the stream is too deep to cross.

In other words, it's no superhighway, just an old-fashioned kind of a road following the curves and contours
of the country the way roads used to do before we learned
how to move the mountains out of the way. On the other
hand, the pavement is new enough not to have acquired
too many potholes, and wide enough that you can meet a
big semi without taking to the ditch. Actually, it's kind of
a fun road to drive if you like to use your machinery
hard, sports car-fashion; and we made pretty good time
in the husky carryall. We were in the real desert Baja
now, and there were few communities to slow us down.
There was very little traffic. The only driving problem was
caused by the occasional cows, goats, and burros wandering along the unfenced right-of-way and across it, as if
they owned the country, and perhaps they did. Certainly
there seemed to be very few humans around to claim it.

We reached the next El Presidente establishment in
time for an early lunch, ate, and kept going. It wasn't re-

ally spectacular country—there were no tall, snow-capped peaks or vast, deep canyons—but it just had to be, I decided, the densest, biggest cactus garden on earth. We wiggled through a small range of hills and came out on the shore of what seemed to be a tremendous old lake, now dry. It ran off into the distance, gleaming white out there with, presumably, the salt or alkali left behind when the last water evaporated. The next roadside sign pointed to a town off to the right called, without a great deal of originality, Laguna Seca—dry lagoon to you.

I hit the brakes abruptly. Something was stirring in my mind. Clarissa glanced at me but had sense enough to refrain from asking questions. I was remembering a sentence that had struck me as strange during one of my telephone conversations with Mac—those exercises in reverse doubletalk for the benefit of Mr. Euler's electronic snoopers. Speaking of Norma, Mac had said: *It isn't likely that her investigation of Ernemann would have led her . . . to that desolate dried-up seabottom known as the great Southwest.*

My chief isn't exactly what you'd call a plainspoken man. In fact, he can get flowery as hell sometimes, and this could have been one of the times. Still, he'd been trying to pass me information without tipping off the eavesdroppers. It wasn't smart to take anything for granted. He'd strained hard to get a desolate dried-up seabottom into the conversation, and here, on the only land route available into southern Baja, was a desolate dried-up seabottom.

"The gauge is getting a bit low," I said. "Let's see if they've got some gas in this Laguna Seca place."

"All right," said Clarissa. "I'm not nosy. Don't tell me if you don't want to."

I grinned at her, and made a U-turn and headed back to the intersection, and took the dirt road up through the cactus forest. The town wasn't far, less than a mile, under a low ridge. Apparently it had been on the old road but had been bypassed by the highway. It consisted of half a dozen shacks, a little grocery store—the word is *ab-barotes*—and a single, battered gas pump selling the lower grade of Pemex gas. I didn't particularly want the stuff in my tank. Even the top Mexican juice isn't the best fuel you ever tried to burn. However, I wanted a little time to look and be looked at, so I pulled up and told the boy who came out of the grocery to fill her up.

Then I stomped around a bit as if getting the driving kinks out of my muscles, making certain that if anyone was watching from inside one of the buildings, or up on the ridge, they'd be able to recognize me if they knew me. Nothing happened. Well, it had been only a hunch, and it doesn't ever pay to ignore your hunches in this business; but following them doesn't always pay off, by any means. Nobody tailed us away from there that I could see. The cheap grade of gas knocked like hell the rest of the day.

A little before dusk we reached the 28th parallel of latitude, a very significant geographic line in this part of the world. Here, in the arid middle of nowhere—like Laguna Seca, the nearby town of Guerrero Negro had been bypassed by the new road—was a city-type traffic circle surrounding an enormous, stylized eagle: the monument marking the boundary between *Baja California Norte* and *Baja California Sur*. There was also another good Presidente hotel, this one with reservations for *Señor* and *Señora* Helm. If Ramón ever decided to quit his dangerous profession, I reflected, he'd make a good travel agent or tour director.

"Well," said Clarissa at dinner, "that was certainly a lot of dessicated real estate decorated by a lot of screwy vegetables. What did you say the tall, skinny cacti were called—if they were cacti? Cactuses?"

"They were cirios," I said. "Boojum trees to you."

"I'm a little disappointed," she said. "It really wasn't so very different from Arizona; just a little more prickly growing stuff is all. I thought Baja was supposed to be more spectacular than that."

"I guess the old road was spectacular," I said. "Anything looks spectacular when you're crawling along a dirt track a million miles from nowhere with a good chance of dying of thirst and starvation if you break down."

She was silent for a little. She'd showered and put on a long dress she'd bought in Ensenada, a gaudy, sleeveless sheath of some fairly rough cloth. Unlike the unfortunate pants-and-shirt outfit, it fit very well, and gave her body a magnificent, barbaric look that went oddly but interestingly with her rather sweet and innocent face. I saw her glance towards the windows.

"It's getting dark," she said.

I said, "The man at the desk told me there are some old docks just beyond the town on the Estero San Jose— estuary to you—where we might be able to catch a glimpse of some *ballenas* if we hurry. That is, if you're still interested in whales."

She didn't look at me. She said, "Well, as a matter of fact, I saw a whale once, from a cruise ship."

I said, carefully expressionless, "Sure. If you've seen one whale, you've seen them all."

She glanced at me quickly. After a moment, she blushed. If any whales came into the Estero San Jose that evening, they were not observed by us. . . .

If there's anything I hate, it's directions to places I can't miss. However, apart from pulling that old gag, our tour director had done his job of description well, so well that I'd recognized the turnoff easily when we'd passed it the evening before, about a dozen miles before we reached the hotel.

In the early morning, with the sky light and clear but the sun still below the horizon, we drove back there and made the turn. There was a tiny community that could hardly be called a town, just a handful of scattered mud huts on the desert, west of the road. The side road had been paved that far, presumably when the new highway was built. Beyond the village there was nothing but cactus, and two ruts across the desert leading towards the ocean, invisible to the westward. The road, if you want to call it a road, was solid enough at first but gradually became softer and sandier. I stopped to shift the transfer case into low range so I wouldn't have to waste time doing it if we hit a bad spot and needed lots of power fast. After a quick glance at my watch, sitting there, I looked towards my silent companion.

"Still time to bail out," I said. "Say the word and I'll turn around and run you back to the hotel. You can wait for me there, as I suggested in the first place."

Clarissa studied me curiously. "I thought this was supposed to be just a simple rendezvous to pick up a few things you needed. You're acting as if you expected trouble. Or . . . or is it that you simply don't trust me?"

I grinned. "We will now have Secret Agent Lesson Number One—or is it two, three, or four? Anyway, never use the word 'trust.' Just take it for granted nobody trusts anybody, including you. If you want the truth, I don't trust you. I don't trust you not to get in the way if things get rough. I don't trust you not to get hurt. I don't trust you to do exactly what I tell you—remember the way you kept wandering around against orders back there in the New Mexico hills? Amateurs never figure anybody really means what he says."

Clarissa said, "I promise. Cross my heart, sir. This time I'll do precisely what you tell me, sir. But you are expecting trouble, aren't you?"

I sighed. "I'd be a fool not to, wouldn't I? I'm heading out across the bleak and trackless—well, almost trackless—Baja wasteland to pick up, among other things, a rifle to kill a guy with; a gent named Ernemann who's a pro like me. Ernemann knows damned well that if I wasn't stopped in the U.S. by his bank account trick, I'll be right behind him here in Mexico, or maybe even a little ahead, waiting for him. Do you think I'm being overly cautious if

I assume that he'd rather I wouldn't get my hands on that nice, accurate rifle, or live to use it?"

"But how would he know—"

I said, "Unless you know exactly what's going on, Mrs. O, Secret Agent Lesson Number Two says always assume everybody knows everything. . . . I can't talk you into staying behind?"

"No."

I shrugged and put the truck into gear, and drove it away from the just-appearing sun towards the Pacific Ocean, or an arm of it entitled Laguna de la Muerte, the Lagoon of Death. Whose death, the road map didn't say.

I know something about coaxing a two-wheel-drive vehicle as far as it will go, but we were soon beyond that point. As the ruts got deeper and the sand softer I couldn't help worrying a little. I hoped Ramón knew what he was doing, sending me here. I really had no good notion of what a big 4x4 like mine could do in that stuff. I hoped he did, and hadn't been thinking in terms of the little jeep-type jobs with the big, fat tires. Then the terrain hardened a little, and we came to the first junction Ramón had told me about. I stopped and got out and studied the double goat-track coming up from the south. I got back in, shaking my head.

"Nobody's come that way in the last day or two," I said, sending the truck westwards once more. We still had caught no glimpse of ocean ahead; apparently the coastal dunes blocked the view. After a moment, I said idly, "I wonder what's happened to the boy scout?"

"Who?"

"You remember Euler's boy, Gregory Kotis. Remember how I told him I could track a clean fly across dirty wallpaper?"

"I remember. Why should anything have happened to him?"

"Things happen to people who know too much," I

said. "I wouldn't want to be the one to insure Mr. Kotis' life unless he's very, very careful. I warned him before I sent him back; but like I just told you, amateurs never figure anybody means what he says, and that goes for a lot of Security men. . . . Hang on!"

We dropped into a sudden gully and lunged up the other side. Now the track wound through low sand hills partially covered by some tough, sparse, undernourished brush that squealed along the sides of the carryall in the tight spots. We ground up a ridge and slithered down beyond and stopped at a small lagoon—not Laguna de la Muerte, which covers roughly fifteen miles one way and two or three the other. This was only a narrow, reedy, muddy black puddle running east and west a couple of hundred yards. The dunes were higher beyond, and as I sat there something crawled across the back of my neck. I cut the wheel hard left, hit the gas, sent the blue-and-white monster roaring into the shelter of the nearest dune, and slammed to a stop.

"You don't have to be so impulsive," Clarissa protested, patting her hair back into place. "What's the matter? The road went down the other side of the pond, the right side. I saw the tracks. . . ." She stopped.

"Yeah," I said. "The tracks."

I rubbed the back of my neck, and there was of course nothing there. It had been just the good, old warning buddy-you're-a-beautiful-target feeling. I got out and, keeping under cover, went back and looked out onto the muddy open flat at the near end of the black pool. One look was enough. I hurried around to the other side of the carryall, yanked open the door, and reached into the glove compartment for my second gun, the Colt I'd taken off Gregory Kotis and neglected to return.

"Out you go," I said to Clarissa. "We're taking to the brush. Stay with me, and if I say down, you *down;* I don't care if it's in the middle of a cactus or a mud puddle. Come on. . . ."

fourteen ....

We struggled up the back of a dune and found a neat, brushy hollow just over the top that would, I thought, provide adequate cover for one person. The early-morning chill was leaving the desert as the sun rose, and the face Clarissa turned to me was shiny under the floppy, fashionable hat that now showed stains of perspiration along the band. Her blouse hung open limply, and she'd snagged a knee of her slacks. It was hard to remember the painfully neat, painfully timid woman in the air-conditioned Lincoln.

"Well, I hope this one is satisfactory," she panted, a big, healthy, sexy girl who'd been hiking hard. "I don't know how many more little sand mountains I'm good for . . . Matthew!"

"What's the matter?"

"This is no time for *that!*"

"Well, button your goddamned blouse, then," I said.

She buttoned it and tucked it in, smiling faintly. "Some time you'll have to tell me what's so stimulating about a disheveled wench in the last throes of exhaustion; but right now I'd like to know what the hell we're looking for."

"We're trying to find a nice, comfortable place in which to wait for somebody to come and kill us," I said.

"I'm sorry I asked."

"You'll be glad we spent a little time looking when the fireworks start," I said. "This is your private cozy womb right here. I'll take the last one we inspected, back over there."

I was pulling off my shirt as I spoke. It was one of the loose cotton garments I'd picked up in Ensenada as more suited to the lowland climate of Baja than the heavy wool number I'd worn for Santa Fe and the high country farther north. This was a picturesque shirt such as they turn out for the tourists, blue with red embroidery, veddy, veddy native indeed. No native would have been caught dead in it, but I'd figured, with my well-broken-in jeans, it had made pretty good tourist camouflage. Now I arranged it carefully among the bushes a couple of yards from Clarissa's natural foxhole, showing just a glint of blue from a distance, I hoped.

"Okay, that's me," I said. "I'm lying in wait for them there, understand? I'm a real sneaky type, and I've circled around to watch my back trail—you can see it down there in the sand, the track we made before we turned. Of course, they're smarties too, and they'll be expecting an ambush; but just so they don't slip up and overlook me, I want you to shake that bush over there a bit, every two or three minutes. No more often and not hard. Don't overdo it and don't reach up too high and expose yourself. If there's shooting, just hunker down and stay perfectly still. Don't do *anything* more, no matter how bright it may seem to you at the time. Just stay under cover. I'll get back to you, I promise. Do you think you can manage all that?"

"Yes, but what makes you so sure somebody—"

"Hell, you saw the tracks," I said.

"So there's a car ahead of us. Isn't that what you expected?"

"No. Ramón was supposed to cover from behind and make sure we weren't followed. Then he was supposed to come in after us."

"A camper or fisherman?"

"Batting around the boondocks in the dark?"

"How do you know he came in the dark?"

"He cut the mud too close and almost got stuck; he wouldn't have made that mistake with good visibility. But he intended to leave tracks for me to see. Otherwise he'd have parked somewhere else and slipped in on foot. That means, probably, that there was a gun on us when we drove up to that little lagoon. He didn't shoot because nailing a guy inside a car isn't quite surefire. He was hoping I'd get out to take a look, so he could take me in the open while I was making like Tracker Helm, the human bloodhound. Then I swung the truck around fast and drove where he hadn't expected so all he could get was you, and he didn't want you, particularly."

"Gee," she said, "Thanks awfully. Well, I always wanted to see a superspy in action, but it still seems pretty vague to me. After all, we haven't heard or seen a sign of life since we arrived."

"Don't worry about the signs of life, Mrs. O," I said. "It's the signs of death that concern us. Remember, keep down. Never mind if all hell breaks loose. Stay *down*. Now assume the position and let's see how much protection you have. . . ."

I left her lying there in the sand, and made my way to my own vantage point about fifty yards back towards the ocean, the direction from which I expected them to come unless they got very fancy indeed. My shelter wasn't as good as Clarissa's, but I hoped I wouldn't need it as badly. I checked my watch. Twenty minutes had passed since we'd left the carryall. Well, their ambush had failed;

their quarry was alerted; they wouldn't commence the pursuit without a council of war. Then they'd move slowly, cautiously, first making sure there was nobody left around my truck to take them from behind. After all, if they knew anything, they knew they were after carnivorous game that had been known to bite back. If all I'd wanted was to get clear safely, I'd simply have motored to hell out of there across country. I didn't think the fact would have escaped them.

Another twenty minutes passed before I heard one. They were taking their time. I didn't blame them. That brushy, knobby, sandy coastal landscape was great ambush country. At last, watching the place where Clarissa's tracks and mine, just blurred depressions in the sand, crossed a little ridge to the right before swinging down below me, I saw a dark head lift cautiously among the scraggly bushes. The face was quite dark, also. It wasn't Ernemann unless he'd used a lot of hair dye and makeup, and what would be the point of a disguise here?

The range was too long for a certain revolver shot, and I had to make sure of my target. After all, Ramón could conceivably have changed the signals without telling me and driven in ahead. It would have been a stupid, dangerous thing for him to do, and I didn't really think he'd pull such a jackass stunt, but I didn't want to take even a remote risk of burning down some honest Mexican agents by mistake. I saw my man draw back, and I saw the brush stir slightly as he started to move my way.

This was the tracker. There would be at least one flanker, I figured, covering him from one side or the other as he worked out the trail. Maybe I was flattering myself a bit, but I didn't figure anybody would send just one man to do a job on a gent from a known specialist outfit like ours. Then I had the flanker spotted, too, or one of them; he was coming right up the slot from the ocean towards my private dune. The tracker had stopped abruptly. He had it now; the bush that moved in the dead calm of early morning, the little touch of cheerful blue in the bleak desert. . . .

He gave me no more worries about identity. He simply hurled himself aside and, prone, sent a prolonged burst from his machine pistol into the patch of brush over there. Probably he thought that I'd kicked the bush by mistake as I braced myself to shoot—that he was saving his own life by firing first. I hoped Clarissa was following instructions for a change and keeping her head down. The bullets sprayed a lot of sand around over there, and it looked as if I'd have to break out another of my new shirts when I got back to the hotel. He had that one pretty well centered.

It was a toss-up which way he'd go when he let up on the trigger, and I got the break. He came my way, crouching low and racing for a hollow that would cover him from Clarissa's direction. Lying above and behind him, I led him like a deer and dropped him nicely. At once, I rolled aside and let myself continue to roll down the sandy slope like a kid playing games on the beach, as all hell broke loose. The flanker was chewing up my recently vacated hilltop with another squirt gun. I hadn't really known he'd got behind me—I'd lost him for a couple of minutes while I was watching the other—but with him missing, it just hadn't seemed smart to hang around and admire my marksmanship.

I picked myself up and ran around the dune and caught him coming off his own little hilltop back there, a smallish dark man, again no Ernemann. He tried to put on the brakes but the sand betrayed him. He sat down, sliding; and I fired twice and connected once, but the range was long and it wasn't a very good hit, just good enough to make him let go the chopper in a moment of shock. He made a stab to reclaim it, but realized he'd be dead in another second, and ran for cover instead, limping heavily. I tried for him twice and saw sand kick up short once and to the side once. Lousy. I could blame it on shortness of breath and uncertain footing, I suppose. The count was five. He turned and shot at me with some kind of a pistol, one-handed, like target practice, but he wasn't doing any better than I was. With five gone, my S & W was empty. By the time I'd hauled out the Colt I'd taken from Gregory Kotis in another country and another lifetime, I had no mark visible in that direction.

Grimacing, I moved cautiously back around my dune, working upwards, to where I could see the first man again. He'd sprawled headlong when hit, gun way out ahead of him, but now he was curled up in a tight ball at the foot of the sandy slope and no weapon was in sight. Cute. I sat down and put my elbows on my knees and cocked the revolver and aimed carefully, two-handed; but when the hammer fell, the bullet hit the sand beside him, short. Either Kotis had never bothered to sight in his piece, or the BIS boys used a totally different sight picture from ours—of course, my mistake was in not checking the gun, but, not really expecting to use the borrowed piece I hadn't. When I got out of this, if I got out of it, I intended to mark my calendar with a new holiday: Incompetence Day.

However, my near miss had stung my target into action. He was rearing up painfully, swinging the ugly little squirt gun my way. I used about eighteen inches of Kentucky windage—well, Kentucky elevation—to compensate for Kotis's peculiar sighting system. The shot was good, and I gave the guy another as he collapsed, just to make absolutely sure he didn't get up and bother the lady while I was gone.

I would have liked to get his chopper, or the other one, but I didn't think I had that much time. I ran oceanwards, reloading both revolvers as I ran, a neat trick that cost me three dropped cartridges. There was blood on the sand ahead of me. I gambled that, wounded and alone, the fleeing man would give up his assassination project as a lost cause and head straight for his escape vehicle instead of pulling some kind of ambush. I gambled that nobody'd taken time to disable or booby-trap my carryall. I gambled that it was the biggest buggy around. I won the first two bets. Nobody shot at me as I raced heedlessly for the truck, and it started instantly and didn't blow up. I rammed the transfer case lever all the way forward, as the salesman had instructed, locking everything up tight for maximum traction. I backed out into the open, swung around, and headed down the telltale tire tracks that followed the north edge of the lagoon. When they curved back into the dunes, I followed them.

My bullet had slowed my quarry. He hadn't quite made it to his transportation when my big 4WD truck came bouncing and crashing into sight. He threw a glance my way and scrambled frantically up a sandy slope towards a vehicle parked on the brushy ridge above; a spot selected, presumably, to overlook the lagoon and the road. I remembered that the far slope was quite steep. The car was one of the jazzy little 4x4 Ford products named after an unruly horse. I'd won my third bet. It was only about half the size of my three-ton tank. If a demolition derby ensued, I had the edge.

The fleeing man reached his goal. I saw the door close; but I was already putting the carryall to the slope. Hell, if that little thing could make it, we could—I hoped. The long truck went roaring up there like a large dog clawing and scratching his way over a gate. Before the driver could get his motor started, my massive front bumper had caught the rear of his vehicle. There was a moment when I wondered if we had power and traction enough to do the job; but the carryall kept moving inexorably with everything screaming and grinding away, and bulldozed the Bronco right over the edge. I slammed to a stop on the ridge from which it had just departed and jumped out with my gun ready.

The little boondocks Ford was sliding down the steep

face of the dune below me. The driver still hadn't managed to get his motor started. As I watched, the rear end started to go right. It was only a slight angle at first, but it got greater. When the vehicle came almost crosswise to the slope it fell onto its right side, rolled over onto its top, flopped clear over onto its left side, and slid the rest of the way like that, stopping only when the slope flattened out towards the lagoon.

After a little, the upper door opened and a hand with a gun emerged. My flanker friend climbed out—well, started to climb out. I was rested and ready, sitting up there comfortably with my elbows on my knees and both hands on the gun, my own gun. It was time I did a little respectable shooting for a change, and I did it.

fifteen ••••••••••••••••••••••••••

Ramón said, "It is not necessary to kill everyone, *Señor* Helm. We are tolerant; we do not require total annihilation. It is permitted to leave alive a small fraction of the population of Baja California. . . . You say there is another dead body inland? I presume you shot him in cold blood like this one. Just like target practice from the top of this little hill, very safe!"

He wasn't very happy with me, maybe because, instead of scrambling down to him, I'd made him climb up the sandy ridge to me. I'd had my morning exercise; it was time he got his.

"Safe," I said. "Sure. But not as safe as you, *amigo,* carefully waiting a couple of miles away for the shooting to stop. You were supposed to be covering me, remember?"

I wasn't very happy with him, either. Down below us, his driver was investigating the capsized Bronco and the dead man draped over the side of it. Nearby stood the staff car in which they'd just arrived, a big, boxy, four-wheel-drive station wagon of Japanese manufacture:

Toyota's answer to the larger Land Rover. It had a whip antenna indicating two-way radio communications.

I said, "Two men with choppers, and me with a couple of little one-hand guns, and you're complaining because I made sure of the bastards? What the hell do you think this is, anyway, some kind of a sporting event? They did their best to kill me. They had their chance. Just because they muffed it, was I supposed to turn them loose to try again? That guy inland, for instance—he totally ruined a perfectly good shirt he thought was me, and he may actually have got Mrs. O'Hearn, I didn't have time to check. Just how much does a guy have to do to earn a quick, rough departure around here, anyway?"

Ramón didn't reply directly. "That is another thing," he said. "The magnificent *Señora* O'Hearn. Why did you bring her? It was not in the instructions—"

"You didn't say not to, and she wanted to come. I have a hunch she changed her mind a little while ago, but that's her problem, not yours." I drew a long breath. "Tell your boy to stop right there, Ramón."

"What?"

"Your driver. He's coming this way. I don't want him any closer."

"But I do not understand—"

I said harshly, "You understand all right. Why are you so concerned about two dead killers? I've seen you act pretty cold-blooded about a number of stiffs in the past; why do these upset you so? Could it be that these well-armed gents waiting for me here were good friends of yours. . . . I mean it! One step more and the crap hits the propeller! Stop him *now!*"

Ramón looked at me hard. Then he made a small gesture with his hand. The man who'd started climbing towards us stopped moving. Then we stood there for a while. A small breeze had come up. Off to the right, the wide expanse of Laguna de la Muerte was visible at last, beyond a few more dunes and a wide, flat, grayish beach that looked to be more mud than sand. It looked bleak and hostile, the Lagoon of Death, and I wondered who'd died to name it. Probably some poor, damned sailors or fishermen. Well, we were keeping right up with the old tradition.

"You had better say what you are thinking." Ramón spoke very softly. "It is better in the open. *Por favor.*"

I said, "I am thinking that some very fancy explanations are in order, *Señor* Solana-Ruiz. I run into a deadfall. I fight my way out of it. And my good friend and professional associate, who set up the rendezvous, who promised to protect me, comes roaring up after it's all over and raises hell with me for hurting those two poor little innocent would-be murderers. . . . Goddamn it, Ramón, keep your boy still!" I let my hand come to rest on the Smith and Wesson in my waistband. "Or, hell, let him come. Call in the Rurales. Call in the army and the navy. Go ahead, damn you. It's your game; you set it up. Second quarter coming up. Blow the goddamn whistle and let's play ball, only you won't live to see who wins. . . . Ah, hell!"

I drew another long, shaky breath. It was reaction, I guess. It hits that way sometimes. Ramón smiled faintly and turned his head.

"Amado," he called. *"Dos cervezas. Pronto."*

The man below turned and made his way to the Toyota, reached inside, and started back with a bottle in each hand. Ramon looked at me.

"Shall I let him approach, now?"

"Oh, hell, yes," I said. "The more the merrier. The closer he comes, the easier I can shoot him. But you've probably got that beer poisoned, anyway."

"Do you really think I would send you into a trap?"

"Cut it out," I said. "Let's not be childish. I know damned well you'd send me into a trap if it suited your purposes. I'd do the same for you." When he didn't speak, I went on: "Give me a reasonable alternative.

Who else is there? Nobody. Neither of those dead men resemble Ernemann in any way except in their prefer-ence for automatic firepower. Well, he could have sent them, sure, but how would he know where? The girl asked the question a while ago. I kind of brushed her off, but it's a damned good question. You're the only one who knew I was coming here. Those boys didn't follow me in. They'd been told where to make their ambush. They were here before dawn, waiting for me."

The driver had made it over the rim. He was a swarthy, tough-looking individual with the short legs, and the big shoulders and chest, of a moderately hairless go-rilla. The glance he threw me wasn't friendly. He held out a beer to Ramón.

"If you will excuse me," Ramón said, taking the bottle. He put it to his lips and drank, and gave it to me. "So. If there is poison, we die together."

"Salud y pesetas," I said, taking a swig. "I'm still wait-ing to hear whose chopper-types those were if they weren't yours."

"Perhaps Amado found something on the body that will throw light on the subject." He spoke to the dark-faced driver, who took a wallet from his shirt pocket and passed it over. Ramón flipped it open, and glanced at me, and held it out. "Does that help, *amigo?*"

I took the open wallet and looked at the ID card dis-played under a neat plastic window. It indicated that the late owner had been a gent by the name of John Ferdi-nand Ortiz, a special operative of the Bureau of Internal Security of the United States Department of . . .

"One of Euler's boys!" I said, whistling softly. "Wan-dering through foreign lands with a homicidal friend and two very illegal automatic weapons. I don't believe it! Andrew must have flipped. Who does he think he is, the CIA?"

"You bluffed *Señor* Euler at the border, remember?" Ramón said. "You made him let you through; you made him look foolish. That is something some men never forgive."

I sighed. "One apology coming up. *After* you tell me how they knew enough to be here at the right spot at the right time."

Ramón threw a glance inland. "I think you know the answer, Matthew."

"O'Hearn? But how the hell would she know——"

"You did not speak of our rendezvous? You gave no hints?"

"No . . . wait a minute. I did say something about meeting you down a dirt road in the morning. And I guess I did slow down passing the intersection yesterday, and maybe I looked around to make sure it was the right one and I'd recognize it coming the other way." I frowned. "But say she put it together, how did she get the message out? She wasn't out of my sight. . . . Well, I suppose she did answer the call of nature once or twice without company, and so did I. She could have slipped something to somebody or left a message where it could be found. But what would be her motive in selling me to Euler, the guy who shot her brother?"

"For that," said Ramón, "I think we had better consult the lady. After we finish our beer."

I did some work on the contents of my bottle. I said thoughtfully, "There is just one little thing."

"What is that little thing, Matthew?"

"It would be very convenient if said lady should die, now that you've decided she's guilty as hell. I mean, you can blame dead people for just about anything, can't you?"

"Do you think I would——"

"You or your man Friday. Remember the old *ley de fuga* and where it was invented. I don't want her mowed down just because she panics and starts to run, or something." I finished my beer and handed the bottle to Amado, who looked at it with disdain and tossed it into the bushes. Well, it was his country. If he wanted it littered with broken glass, I could hardly object. I said, "I think I'd like your gun, Ramón, before I lead you to her. Just temporarily, of course. And *Señor* Amado's also. And we'll walk it from here, just in case there's spare artillery in your car. Okay?"

I waited. After a reasonable number of seconds had passed, Ramón grinned abruptly. "You are not a very trusting man."

I said, "I'm here. I'm alive. I'll be trusting as hell after I retire."

"You, my friend, will never retire. You enjoy too much gambling with your life. One day you will lose, but you will never retire. . . . Here."

I took the automatic pistol he gave me, and the one yielded up reluctantly by chesty, short-legged Amado. By the time I had them tucked away, added to my own dual armamentation, I was weighted down with firearms to the point where my own legs had, I figured, diminished at least an inch from sheer compression.

"This way, gents," I said.

It was not far as I remembered it. I'd been afraid I wouldn't recognize the place—one brushy dune looks pretty much like another—but I brought them right to the opening of the cozy, familiar, little sandy valley with a dead man in it. My blue shirt was still visible among the bushes on the hill beyond, but there were no signs of life and something was missing. For the second time, the dead man's machine pistol had vanished, although this time he had not changed position since my last bullet hit him.

I grimaced, glancing towards Clarissa's hideout. *Don't do anything more, no matter how bright it may seem,* I'd told her, but she'd never been a girl for obeying instructions to the letter.

"Wait here," I said to Ramón. "We'd better not go charging up there in a bunch. I think the lady's got herself a stuttergun up there. She's been shot at today for the first time in her life. She may be slightly nervous."

"Or slightly guilty," Ramón said.

"I've heard your theory," I said. "I'm giving it due consideration. . . . Well, here goes." I stepped forward and yelled, "Clarissa! Hey, Mrs. O'Hearn. It's me, Matt. Hold everything, I'm coming in."

Nothing stirred; nobody answered. Still more or less outside the danger zone, I took time to select my route carefully, past the dead man and the little hollow he'd picked for shelter but had never reached, and thence to the base of Clarissa's dune where a sandy ridge ought to give me a little cover. I mean, a frightened girl with a machine pistol—or a guilty one, if Ramón was right— isn't anything you want to approach without due care and forethought. The fact that she hadn't answered my call was indication enough that something was wrong.

I started forward. "Hey, Mrs. O," I shouted. "Everything's okay. You can relax; the war's over. . . ."

I saw movement up there, and I drew a breath of relief. She was coming out of her hole. She was standing up. She was . . .

I took three long steps and flung myself down behind the dead man as the automatic weapon in her hands started to chatter wickedly. Inexperienced, she was having trouble controlling it, and the bullets were spraying everywhere, but one made a solid hit on the body sheltering me; I felt it jerk with the impact. The burst seemed to go on forever with sand spurting up here and there all around me, then the clip went empty. The firing stopped, leaving a ringing silence. I heard an odd, distant, gasping sound. The girl on the hill was crying. I raised my head cautiously.

"No!" she sobbed. "Oh, no, no, no, please no, I don't want to die! Please don't. . . ."

She hurled the empty weapon away from her and

turned and ran. I scrambled to my feet and raced—well, as fast as you can race in soft sand—around the left of the dune. My immediate fear was that she'd seen where the second chopper had fallen, earlier, and was going for it. However, when I caught sight of her, she was heading the other way, inland, slipping and sliding down the slope and then running like a deer after reaching level ground. I could hear her sobbing hysterically as she ran, but the hysterics didn't slow her noticeably. My pockets were full of other people's firearms that didn't help my speed a bit. At last, throwing a panicky look over her shoulder, she missed a step and fell headlong. I threw myself on top of her and pinned her down.

"No," she babbled, "no, no, no, don't kill me. . . ."

"That's enough, Mrs. O," I said. "Nobody's going to kill you. Now stand up and blow your nose and tuck your shirttail in again; you look like hell."

I waited until she stopped fighting me, and got off her, and stood up. She lay there a moment longer. At last she turned her head warily and peeked at me through the wild tangle of her hair.

"Matt? But I thought . . . Oh, my God!"

"Come on, get up." I reached down and helped her rise. "Do you make a habit of flipping your wig like that?"

"What do you expect?" She didn't look at me, and her voice was sullen. "Did . . . did you know how it was going to be when you put me there?"

"I told you there might be some shooting."

"Some shooting! You didn't say it was going to be a . . . a pitched battle. When that machine gun went off and the bullets started hitting all around me and whistling and screaming and kicking sand all over me I really thought I was going to . . . I was *sick* I was so scared! And then there was more shooting, and then after a long, long time still more shots far away, and I knew they'd killed you and would be coming for me and I ran down and got the gun and waited . . . waited . . . Did I shoot at you? Why didn't you call and tell me you were there? I didn't recognize . . . If I'd known it was you . . ."

"I did call," I said.

She shook her head. "I didn't hear a thing. All I could hear was my heart beating, kind of roaring in my ears. I just saw *them* coming, three of them, and one sneaking forward to kill me. . . ."

"Sure."

Abruptly, she started doing the usual feminine things to her disheveled hair and disordered clothes. Without looking at me, she said, "Well, all right, go ahead and say it! Jack used to say it. The only thing worse than a coward, he'd say when I wouldn't ride a mean horse or ski a steep slope or something . . . the only thing worse than a coward is a *big* coward."

"Dear Brother Jack," I said. "You sure picked the men in your life. Well, there's another coming, a handsome Latin type, and I'm afraid he's going to arrest you, Mrs. O."

"*Arrest* me!" she gasped. "But why?"

"Well, he has some odd theories about you, and I'm afraid he's thinking that you just confirmed them with all that shooting. Since I'm not at all certain he isn't right, and since he's got the authority here and I haven't, I guess I'll just have to let him take you."

sixteen ....

I managed to back the carryall off the steep, sandy ridge without rolling it over, but I had a couple of uneasy moments before I got it to the bottom, right side up. I promised myself that as soon as I could spare a little time I'd find myself a private piece of desert to practice on, so I'd know what I was doing with the big machine.

The Toyota was waiting for me on the road at the head of the lagoon. Ramón stood beside it with a cased rifle slung over one shoulder and a couple of boxes of cartridges in his hand. There had been some talk of fishing tackle, but I didn't see any and I didn't ask. Ramón came forward, laid the rifle carefully in back, and got in beside me.

"Just a minute," I said.

I picked up the purse Clarissa had left on the seat and took it over to her. Actually, I had to reach through the open window and place it on her lap. She didn't acknowledge my presence in any way. Somebody'd found her hat and given it back to her, and she'd pulled it down hard so I couldn't really see her face, and it probably wouldn't have done me much good, anyway. Reading minds and characters isn't really what I do best.

Amado drove the Toyota away. It was a hell of an ugly, slab-sided vehicle, unlike my sexy boondocks glamor buggy with its pretty tweed upholstery and two-tone paint. Well, pretty or not, the big Chevy had done exactly what I'd asked of it. I had no grounds for complaint. I paused in front of it to check for damage, and found only a couple of scratches in the chrome of the front bumper. I got in beside Ramón and watched the Toyota disappear out of sight.

"Are you sure he can handle her all alone?" I asked sourly. "She's a big, strong girl."

"Amado will take care of her."

"That's just what I'm afraid of."

Ramón glanced at me. "Do not fear; she will come to no harm, I promise you. With our current political difficulties we cannot afford to hurt the wealthy and influential *Señora* O'Hearn from the powerful *Estados Unidos.* In fact, I want to thank you for your foresight in disarming us; otherwise we would undoubtedly have shot her when she opened fire. It would have created a very embarrassing international situation. You have my gratitude for preventing it."

I said, "Yeah, but you're not grateful enough to tell me about a slight case of revolution you're expecting locally."

There was a little silence; then Ramón laughed. "You know how security is, *amigo,* if anyone does. The lady told you? That means she's in her husband's confidence. Very interesting."

I started the carryall up the rutted track. "It doesn't necessarily follow. She claims she simply overheard some informative conversations."

"Yes. She also claims she didn't recognize you at seventy-five meters. But she was most certainly trying to kill you, no matter what she claims."

"Maybe," I said, "but I knew a scared rookie agent

once who went haywire and massacred two colleagues by mistake, taking them for enemy agents sneaking up on him—just like this, in broad daylight. Hell, Wild Bill Hickock, who could hardly be called a rookie, shot down his own deputy in a moment of stress, when the guy came running into an alley to help right after an attempt had been made on Hickock's life. You never can tell how people are going to react when the guns start going off."

Ramón laughed again. "Could it be that you are simply making chivalrous excuses for the *señora* because you have enjoyed her extramarital favors, *amigo?* You said yourself that she insisted on accompanying you clear from Santa Fe. Her motive is becoming fairly obvious, is it not?"

I didn't answer. I just switched on the air-conditioning against the growing heat. As we topped the first rise, we saw the Toyota a quarter of a mile ahead, bouncing hard on its stiff springs as Amado pushed it along at a good clip. I had a mental picture of the big girl beside him, with her oddly sweet face and her expensive, badly wilted costume, enduring the jolting ride without expression.

"No, no," Ramón went on. "Do not deceive yourself. That is a very cool and clever and dangerous woman. We will hold her until this business is over; but then I am afraid we will have to release her. Unfortunately, prosecution is not practical. It would involve too many awkward public explanations, and it is not, after all, as if she had actually managed to kill you on Mexican soil."

"Sorry about that," I said.

"A number of people will undoubtedly be sorry about it, when they learn of it," Ramón said. "Like your *Señor* Euler."

"I still can't figure that guy," I said. "Incidentally, I didn't get a good look at those machine pistols but they seemed familiar. Did he actually send his flunkies down here waving a couple of U.S. government firearms?"

"No, he is not quite that stupid," Ramón said. "Those

were PAM-1 weapons. A reasonably close copy of your .45 caliber M3 submachine gun, but in the 9mm caliber and manufactured in Argentina. And in case you're interested, the second dead man was a senior special operative for the same bureau, named Ernest Dixon. A very Anglo-Saxon name, I must say, for one who in appearance could easily have passed for Mexican."

I said, "Up in New Mexico, U.S.A., Dixon is often a Spanish name, believe it or not. I know some Dixons up there who can hardly speak English. Well, at least nobody can accuse Andrew of not being an equal-opportunity employer." I grimaced. "All races and sexes. I'd still like to know why the well-heeled Mrs. Oscar O'Hearn would play ball with the man who killed her brother. Well, to hell with it. Let's stop for a little rifle practice, if you don't mind. Not that I don't trust your armorers, Ramón, but I like to do my own sighting-in. While I'm banging away, you can tell me what's next on the agenda. . . ."

He did, and that afternoon I checked in at the Hotel Serenidad, at the mouth of the palm-fringed Santa Rosalia River, just outside the picturesque town of Mulege. It was located in a lush oasis of tropical jungle that was kind of startling after all the long miles of arid Baja landscape. We'd crossed the peninsula from west to east, from the Pacific Ocean to the Gulf of California, and we'd been tailed almost the whole way by a cautious character in a small, shabby-looking station wagon that had never got close enough for me to determine the make or license plate.

Actually, the shadow had picked us up when Ramón and I stopped to have breakfast and pay my bill—and change me into an unventilated shirt—at the El Presidente Hotel where Clarissa and I had spent the night. I'd caught an occasional glimpse of him in the mirrors during the hundred and sixty mile drive, just often enough to be certain he wasn't hanging on back there accidentally. I'd seen no need to mention him to Ramón. Anyway, I was fairly certain that my faithful Mexican friend and loyal undercover ally was quite aware of the surveillance and had, in fact, ordered it. It was a small precaution, I figured, against my getting too independent now that we were getting down into the critical area, and I might as well pretend I didn't notice. I'll admit to a certain feeling of claustrophobia, however. Things were closing in.

The hotel was an older one, with low, stucco cottages grouped around a main building. Its main attraction for us, I gathered, was that before the highway was paved and people could drive here in reasonable comfort, it used to be strictly a fly-in fishing resort with its own airstrip, still in operation. I took my suitcase to the unit assigned to me—I'd been glad to see that the matching bag we'd bought Clarissa had disappeared from last night's hotel room. Apparently Amado had been considerate enough to stop for it on the way to her place of detention, wherever it might be. I washed off some of the sand I still carried from the morning's adventures and went out to find the bar and rejoin Ramón, according to instructions.

The bar was a dark, cool building, empty except for the bartender, Ramón, and a stocky individual who had the well-tanned but fleshy look of the kind of successful American businessman who plays hard in the sun when he's not making money, but not hard enough to work off everything he eats. It surprised me to hear him conversing in fluent Spanish, a hell of a lot better than my own clumsy border lingo. I didn't ask if I could join them at their table; I just walked past to the bar and ordered a martini. I guess a Margarita would have reminded me of something I preferred to forget; I was a little fed up with romantic Mexico and its romantic cactus juice.

"Join me, *amigo*," Ramón said, behind me.

The American, if he was an American, was gone. I took my drink over there and sat down. "I didn't want to intrude," I said.

"A friend of mine," Ramón said. "He had information for us. Things are happening fast. You should know that we are actually one day behind General Hernando Díaz and his good Yankee friend, *Señora* O'Hearn's husband Oscar. They were here yesterday in O'Hearn's plane with its handsome *piloto*. They conferred with certain people here in Mulege, and in Santa Rosalia, forty miles to the north. Today they are having similar conferences in Loreto, sixty miles south. Tomorrow they will be in La Paz."

I said, "It doesn't sound as if they're getting much fishing done."

Ramón shook his head. "Since you are now aware of the situation, I will not try to convince you that angling was the subject of all these meetings. As you have undoubtedly noticed, I did not even take the trouble to supply you with tackle. It seemed unlikely, with this recent burst of activity, that you would have an opportunity to approach them as a fellow-angler, as we had planned. We will have to work out a new approach. In the meantime, I would like you to stay here. I believe we have a line on Ernemann himself, but I would like to confirm the information. He was supposedly seen leaving La Paz in an automobile heading south. I will fly down there and find out the details."

I said, "There's not a hell of a lot of Baja California south of La Paz, is there?"

Ramón said, "On the contrary, it is almost two hundred kilometers by road from the city of La Paz to Cabo San Lucas, the southernmost tip of the peninsula. There are some big hotels down there catering to tourists and fishermen; it is a fine fishing area. It may be that Ernemann has information about Díaz's plans we do not yet have. It may be that he is driving down there in the expectation that the general will come to him. I will let you know as soon as I have enough information. I am leaving Amado to watch over you, if you do not object. Be ready to leave at a moment's notice. . . . I think that is my airplane landing now. *Adiós, amigo.*"

He hurried out, I didn't follow to see him off. Presently I heard a small plane take off outside.

I had a second martini and decided that was enough for a steel-nerved super agent with a razor-sharp mind that was better kept clear, considering the number of folks who'd declared themselves in favor of my demise—not to mention the ones of the same persuasion remaining undeclared. I signed the check and took a little walk down by the palmy, muddy river. It looked like a good place for alligators, if they have alligators in Mexico, but all the wildlife I really saw was seagulls and some long-legged white shorebirds, egrets perhaps. The short-legged gent trailing along behind I considered more on the order of a domestic animal, which of course didn't make him any less dangerous. After all, statistics show that the deadliest beast on the North American continent is the ordinary domestic dairy bull.

I wondered where Amado had deposited Clarissa O'Hearn for safekeeping before coming here to keep an eye on me. I sighed, wishing I had a simple system for telling the good guys from the bad guys. Not to mention the girls. I headed back to the cabin to shower the remaining sand off before dinner. I had the key in the lock when I noticed that the telltale I'd arranged as a matter of routine had been displaced. Somebody'd been through the door since I'd left the room. Perhaps a maid had entered to turn down the beds, except it didn't seem to be that fancy a place, and it was a little early in the day for turning beds, anyway. I was aware that my bodyguard was coming up from the river.

It was a neat problem. If I went in the way one ordinarily enters a hotel room, and somebody was waiting inside I didn't want to see, I could be suddenly dead and Amado would just have the fun of avenging me. On the other hand, if I took the standard room-entering precautions, and there was somebody inside I did want to see, my antics would betray that person's presence to my husky guardian. . . . As I hesitated, there was a small knocking sound from inside the door: three light taps followed by two. I drew a long breath and marched inside.

"Close the door quickly, *estupido!*" It was a low whisper from the shadows to my right.

"Hi, Norma, it's about time you showed up," I said.

seventeen ....

Our girl in Baja, Virginia Dominguez, was smaller than I remembered her. After the company I'd been keeping she looked tiny: a pretty little black-haired, dark-eyed, olive-skinned *señorita*-doll that should have come out of the box complete with a long, full-skirted, Spanish-style dress, a lace mantilla, and a fan.

Actually, she was wearing the kind of white-mottled bluejeans that look as if they'd gone fifteen rounds with a bottle of Clorox, and a red-checked gingham half-blouse. I mean, it was demure and complete as far as it went, with a discreet round neckline and little puffed-up sleeves, but it only went an inch below her breasts. The lower half of the garment was missing, leaving her midriff bare. The pants were so tight above, you wondered if it was safe for her to sit down, but they flared widely below. I could remember when jeans were neat, snug, practical garments suitable for wearing on horseback, but if this girl ever swung a leg over a spooky bronc, with all that piebald denim flapping, she'd get tossed into the nearest clump of cactus.

Here, however, the floppy pantslegs served a useful purpose. As I watched, Norma crouched and drew one leg up, exposing a nicely proportioned little leg decorated with a tricky little sheath, into which she slipped the wicked-looking little knife she had been holding.

"Still the cold-steel girl," I said.

"Go pull the curtains so I can get out of this corner without his seeing me. I'm tired of crawling around on the floor to keep out of range of those windows. Did you know you were being watched?"

I glanced out the window and saw Amado, the human gorilla, leaning against a tree outside, smoking a cigarette. I pulled the draperies and turned back to the little black-haired girl in the corner, wondering how Roger had planned to make use of her, and just what the hell I was supposed to do with her now that I'd found her at last.

I mean, there are certain types of missions that really require a sexy female agent, and others where a good, silent, knife specialist comes in very handy, and still others where just any additional warm body is useful. I couldn't see that any of those conditions pertained. The chances of Ernemann, engaged in an important job, allowing himself to be seduced into helplessness and knifed to death were infinitesimally small; and I could see no other possibilities for Norma to employ her special talents here. I knew she was just barely competent with firearms. Sending her up against an expert chopper-man was simple murder. With an accurate rifle and a little luck I could handle him alone, risking nobody else in the process.

I'd just got rid of the responsibility of one girl, although maybe not exactly the way I'd have liked. I found that I resented being saddled with another—but of course I couldn't afford to let it show.

I switched on the light. "Ramón told me he was leaving his driver to protect me," I said. "He didn't say from what. He also didn't mention a guy who tailed us all the way down from Guerrero Negro—"

"That was no guy, that was me," Norma said. "I'd been keeping pretty far behind you, clear out of sight in fact, until we reached that place with the monument, the 28th Parallel; but when we started getting near civilization, such as it is around here, I figured I'd better close in a bit. Up north, there was no town big enough that I couldn't spot that conspicuous blue bus of yours, just driving through, but I was afraid I might lose you in Santa Rosalia or Mulege."

I watched her walk over to the nearest bed, test it with her fingertips, and confirm the diagnosis with her fanny, bouncing up and down a bit like a kid—but I remembered that she'd once given me convincing proof that she was definitely not a kid. It had been one of those quick hit-and-run things that happen in this racket: a long night of waiting with all preparations made and nothing to do but sweat it out to the crack-of-dawn deadline. I suppose we'd both figured why the hell not—soon we might be dead.

When she looked up at me, tossing the long, glossy black hair back from her small face I saw that she was also remembering the shabby little hotel room in a distant Spanish-speaking city, but there had been no real sentiment involved. It had been simply a brief moment of relaxation in the middle of a tense and dangerous business, nothing to justify a lot of romantic reminiscences. Nevertheless, it was a personal reason, if I needed one, for not risking her life unnecessarily now.

"Not to get inquisitive or anything," she said, "but who's the big, handsome broad you've been hauling around?"

I said, "That's no broad; that's Mrs. Oscar O'Hearn of the Arizona O'Hearnses—you've heard of O'Hearn, Inc. She happens to be Roger's sister."

"I didn't know Roger had a sister."

"I did," I said. "He told me all about her once. She's genuine, all right. He sent her to warn me a few days back when things started getting complicated; and she kind of got more and more involved. You'll be interested to know that her husband is a dear friend of General Hernando Díaz, of whom you may have heard."

Norma wrinkled up her small nose in a way I remembered. "Is that supposed to make sense?" she asked. "You've got the wife and Díaz has the husband—"

I said, "Sweetheart, on this job nothing makes sense. And I haven't got the wife any more. Solana-Ruiz just took her away from me and locked her up somewhere. He thinks she's a very wicked woman, and he may be right."

"Judging by his appearance, he fancies himself as an expert on all kinds of women—I got a good look at him when he had breakfast with you this morning. I don't like those *macho* Latin smoothies, Matt."

I grinned. "Look who's talking about Latin smoothies! What's the matter, you got race prejudice or something, Chicana?"

It was the wrong thing to say. Her eyes narrowed. "Don't call me that!" she snapped. "Let the goddamn pot-smoking U.S. *pachucos* play militant and call themselves Chicanos and talk big about *La Raza—The* Race, for God's sake, as if there was no other! I don't know why the hell other people, like you Swedes for instance, put up with that kind of loudmouthed crap."

I'd forgotten that, like a good many solid U.S. citizens of Spanish descent, she detested the newfangled name that had been foisted on them, she claimed, by a bunch of scruffy activists.

"Who's a Swede?" I asked lightly. "Nobody here but us *Americanos,* honey."

"That's what I mean!" she said. "You don't go around being a professional downtrodden Scandihoovian and yelling about Blonde Power and stuff; why act as if you expected that kind of bullshit from me?"

"Okay, okay," I said. "Simmer down. I apologize for whatever it is I've got to apologize for. . . . Is that why you haven't made contact before, because I had company?"

"Well," Norma said judiciously, "it was an inconvenience, let's say. I didn't know how much you wanted her to know."

"Actually, as I recall, you were supposed to get in touch with Ramón's people by phone."

"*Si, jefe,*" she said. "I do remember the instructions, *jefe,* and I do most humbly apologize for not carrying them out. However, I wasn't too sure about Ramón and his people, either, after something that happened in Tijuana. A couple of well-dressed characters grabbed me right after I crossed the border. They looked like Mexicans, they talked good Spanish, and they acted like cops anywhere in the world. Polite cops, but still cops. After that little encounter with authority, if that's what it was, it didn't seem advisable to make any phone calls until I found out exactly who was screwing whom. I never trust these damn hands-across-the-border deals, anyway."

I looked at her for a moment, remembering two dead men among the sand dunes near Laguna de la Muerte, and the BIS identification I'd been shown.

"I think you may be doing Ramón an injustice," I said. "I don't think those two guys belonged to him. Anyway, they grabbed you in Tijuana, but now you're in Mulege over six hundred miles south. Aren't you leaving something out?"

She shrugged. "Just the old shoelace trick. As I said, they were polite. They couldn't leave the poor little girl tripping over all those nasty trailing strings all the way to the waiting car, could they?"

"You mean, they hadn't frisked you?"

"Oh, sure," she said cheerfully. "They got a hunk of old iron out of my purse, that I carry for just that purpose. A decoy, you might call it. It seems to make men feel they've really accomplished something when they find a gun on a girl. They think they've got the whole problem licked."

I grinned. "And they actually let you bend down and tie your shoes? How innocent can you get? Did you kill anybody?"

She shook her head. "I didn't figure it would be diplomatic, if they were actually Mexican plainclothes operatives of one kind or another. I just flashed the blade at one and he backed off so fast he fell over the other; I guess he's got some prejudice against singing soprano in the local choir. Then I ran like hell. After I'd lost them, well, there's a village called La Jara up there that's practically solid Dominguez. I paid my respects to the senior Mexican members of the family, and borrowed a little Datsun wagon with Baja plates, and headed off to make contact with Roger as ordered. And while we're on that subject, what about Roger?"

"Three guesses," I said. "I'm here, aren't I?"

She was silent for a little; then she sighed. "Well, he wasn't a bad guy for a screwball, but it always scares me to work with a guy who carries a death wish like that. If he wants to get himself spectacularly killed, that's his business; but I don't want to be part of anybody's smoky Götterdämmerung, thanks just the same."

There was another silence. It was time to change the subject. I asked, "How did you find me?"

She said, "You came to the rendezvous at Laguna Seca, didn't you? I'd been lying on the ridge above it so long the birds were nesting in my hair, with a pair of cheap binoculars I'd picked up in Ensenada. I wanted to run down and throw my arms around your beautiful neck, of course, but what with the Tijuana incident, and your lady passenger who wasn't included in the instructions, I decided I'd better just keep myself handy for a day or so, until I could talk with you privately. . . . Matt, what the hell is going on, anyway? How did Roger die? Who were those guys in Tijuana? What was all that shooting off by the sea this morning—I wanted to go in and help, in case you were in trouble, but Ramón was watching the road and that damned little Datsun is no cross-crountry jeep, not in sand, it isn't. I found that out the hard way."

I said, "In theory, of course, we're just routinely tracking down a professional hitman named Ernemann who's annoyed somebody in Washington; or maybe he's simply got too big to be allowed to run loose any longer. In practice, it's got a hell of a lot more involved than a simple touch . . . How about a little mescal while you listen to the long and incomprehensible story?"

I'd said the wrong thing again. She snapped, "Will you for God's sake lay off the condescending racial bit? I drink whiskey and gin just like white folks, Massa Helm!"

"Will you for Christ's sake relax?" I said. "I offered you mescal, Missy Dominguez, because that's what I happened to pick up in Ensenada. If you don't want it, by all means say so, but let's not make a political crisis out of a little booze, huh?"

After a moment, she smiled wryly. "Sorry about that, Matt. Maybe I'm oversensitive. . . ."

It took me about half an hour to bring her up to date. When I'd finished my recital, she held out her glass without speaking, and I poured her another healthy slug, and replenished my own glass more sparingly. After all, I was a couple of martinis ahead of her.

"So you think the men who grabbed me in Tijuana were Andrew Euler's minions," she said thoughtfully. "You think they were planning to take me back into the U.S.? And when they lost me, they set out after you with more drastic intentions?"

"That's the current theory, subject to revisions."

"And I've got twenty grand in my bank account that doesn't belong there?" She threw me a mischievous sideways glance. "Do I get to keep it?"

I grinned. "You're a mercenary bitch. Here are five

more big bills for you to drool over—actually fifty hundreds."

She hesitated, and took the plastic-wrapped package I held out. "What's this for?"

"It's part of Roger's unearned loot, entrusted to me by his sister Clarissa on his instructions. We're supposed to cram it crudely down the throat of whoever set him up, when we learn that person's identity. Spending part of it to make the identification is legitimate, I think, just so there's enough left to choke the guy with."

"Choke, hell," said Norma. "I think the sister handed you an expurgated version, if that's what she told you. That's not where Roger would have said to put it." She studied the wad of bills in its vinyl envelope. "What am I supposed to do with this, really? Spell it out for the dumb little girl, Matt."

I said, "That's just in case you need to bribe somebody, or buy a new car, or something, to get back across the border inconspicuously."

"Across the border?" She stared at me incredulously. "What the hell are you talking about?"

I said, in what I hoped were my most reasonable tones, "We've got to settle some important priorities, doll. We've got troubles ahead of us, sure; but there are big troubles behind, too. Remember, for all practical purposes, we're stateless persons, traitors to our native land. They'll be waiting to grab us any time we try to go home. There's a character up there who hates and detests this organization and is doing his damndest to wipe it out. If we don't pull up our socks and figure out how to deal with him, you and I, right here, he's very likely to succeed.

Norma licked her lips. "You're forgetting, we weren't sent down here to deal with Andrew Euler."

"Right," I said. "But the fact is, Ernemann's pretty much a one-man job. I've handled plenty of guys of Ernemann's caliber all by myself, if I do say so myself. And

I'd like to think somebody was back at the home ranch, preparing the way for my triumphant return."

She looked at me narrowly. "You couldn't be simply sending the dear little girl out of danger, could you?"

I said, "My God, you're hard to live with tonight, Dominguez! One moment I'm a racial bigot and the next I'm a sentimental slob. You know damned well I'd blow your brains out without hesitation if I thought the assignment required a dead female body five feet two. Don't talk nonsense."

She hesitated. "Well, I hate to go running back to the States after chasing you this far, and leave you to tackle the big bad wolf alone."

I was encouraged, but I didn't allow myself to show it. I said, "Don't kid yourself. Ernemann's a cinch compared to what you've got to do. Here, I've got the forces of law and order more or less on my side. Up there, they'll be laying for you. You've got to slip across the border unseen and play detective with every BIS agent in the Southwest looking for you."

She hesitated, and made a face at me. "Okay, you big squarehead, what do I do?"

"Now who's slinging the loaded racial terms?" I paused to get my thoughts together, and went on: "Two things. First, the place where Roger was killed. For some reason, Euler's people are sensitive about it. Find out why. It could be anywhere, I suppose, but I have a hunch it's within a day's drive of Yuma, where Roger was picked up."

"A day's drive from Yuma," she repeated dryly. "That pretty well covers the U.S. from the Pacific to Texas, depending on how fast a driver you're talking about."

"Did I say it was going to be easy?" After a moment, I went on: "The second thing is to find out what really happened in that shoot-out. There are a few discrepancies in the story I got, and I can make some guesses, but we need facts. I think your key is Gregory Kotis. I've already told you about him. He's one of Euler's fair-haired boys, of course, and he was even in on the shooting, but I don't think he feels very good about it. He looks like the original plastic man, BIS model, but he improves on acquaintance. I think he can be reached if you use the right approach. That's assuming you can locate him and he's still alive. If he's dead, you're going to have to find out how and who. . . ."

Ten minutes later I left the cabin and headed for the dining room in the main hotel building. I was aware of my official shadow separating himself from the tree that had been holding him up, and finding himself a comfortable new observation post on the low wall that separated the hotel grounds from the airstrip. From that perch, he could watch the dining room door but he no longer had a view of my cabin. Norma could slip away unseen, which was the general idea.

I felt pretty good about it, like a Boy Scout who'd managed his good deed for the day—but as a matter of fact, it wasn't really a bad idea to have her digging up dirt on A. Euler, since I had no use for her here.

eighteen ....

Inside the building, I found a low, dark, rambling dining room with rustic furniture. There were several tables of sportsmen and sportswomen telling each other big-fish stories in happy, alcoholic voices—mostly U.S. voices. I got a small table by the wall. I was busy studying the menu when the black man in the corner got up and walked out, leaving the sandy-haired gent with the bush jacket sitting alone at the round table back there.

They hadn't looked my way at all, either of them. Nevertheless, the flashing red light came on in the middle of the instrument panel and the warning buzzer sounded. I realized belatedly that I knew the remaining man from somewhere. At least I'd seen a photograph and read through a file, a fairly thick file. The trouble was, all those Great-White-Hunter types look pretty much alike, right down to the squinty, pale blue eyes and the neat little sandy moustache and the prominent front teeth and the affinity for whiskey in impossible quantities. Then I had the name: Huntington. Colonel Peter Walworth Huntington, soldier of fortune, reputedly a very good man to have around if you had a small war to manage, assuming it was a profitable little conflict that would justify his not inconsiderable salary.

Soldiers don't often come within our sphere of interest. We let them shoot each other undisturbed as a rule—but there are exceptions to that rule. I'd studied up on this particular military specimen some years back while preparing for an assignment in a Latin American country farther south. There had been a revolution of sorts going on at the time, of which we disapproved, and we'd heard that Huntington had been hired to assist the insurgent forces in an advisory capacity. As it turned out, I'd managed, with local assistance, to discourage the military coup by disposing of the aspiring strong man before Huntington had a chance to report for duty, so we'd never met; but I remembered reading that the colonel wasn't a very nice man. Well, his business isn't one that attracts very nice people. Neither, I suppose, is mine.

His presence in Baja at this particular time didn't strike me as a tremendous coincidence. After all, Clarissa had suggested, in describing the well-heeled Sanctuary Corporation, that it might invite a few tough mercenaries to its Baja party. However, the colonel's presence in Mulege on the night of my arrival here was stretching coincidence more than I really liked. I ordered dinner and forced myself to relax and wait the situation out, knowing that I'd made the kind of mistake one often doesn't survive in this business. Worrying about a future problem, I'd neglected to concentrate on the present job. I'd been thinking about the situation back home in the U.S.—I'd even dispatched an agent to deal with it—when I should have been concentrating strictly on Baja California Sur.

I hadn't allowed for any serious opposition down here except what might be provided by Ernemann himself. Even after almost walking into a trap at Laguna de la Muerte, I hadn't sat down and really thought things through. Now I was neatly cornered in Mulege. Why Huntington should bother remained to be seen, but I should have anticipated the possibility and been ready for it. After all, you can't poke around a revolution without, sooner or later, meeting a few revolutionaries.

Well, whatever the free-lance military genius in the bush jacket had in mind would undoubtedly become clear with time. Meanwhile, starvation wouldn't improve my position, so I did a thorough job on the fish-of-the-day, washing it down with beer. They do very well with fish down here, and they're not half bad with beer, either. I passed up the dessert-of-the-day, however. It was flan, a national dish that sends a true Mexican into convulsions of ecstasy, but I'd sworn as a kid that when I grew up and could eat anything I wanted, it wouldn't be slimy caramel custard. . . .

The black man had returned while I was eating. In these days of wild and uninhibited Afro hair styles, his neatly shaved head had, somehow, a sinister look. It was a narrow head with a strong, striking, bony face, middle-aged or beyond, on a lanky runner's body. He'd been in the dossier too, I remembered now; apparently he'd been with Huntington a long time. I couldn't recall his name.

I sipped black coffee and watched a third man come in, a small, skinny specimen with a French beret. This one sat down beside Huntington and spoke in his ear and passed him something under the table. They made an odd international trio at the round corner table, quiet and alert among the noisy, boozy, U.S. anglers. I didn't know the little Frenchman, if that was what he was, but I had a hunch that anyone with a ratty, small-eyed, big-nosed face like that wouldn't ever become a bosom pal of mine.

They all ignored me carefully, confirming my feeling that their plans for the evening concerned me closely. I felt a little like a bear up a tree watching the hunters making preparations to shoot him down into the pack of yelping hounds below. Then Huntington stood up deliberately, a lean six-footer, and condescended to look my way at last. He strolled up to my table.

"Don't do anything hasty, old chap," he said. "We have the girl, don't you know?"

He laid a plastic-wrapped package of money on the table in front of me. He put Norma's tricky little leg-sheath, complete with knife, beside it. Scratch one good deed. It occurred to me that I seemed to be losing ladies right and left. Ramón had taken one; now these jokers had another. It was easier thinking of it that way than remembering a hotel room in Mexico City.

I asked, "Do you have her alive or do you have her dead?" My voice, I was glad to hear, sounded nice and expressionless.

Huntington looked distressed. "My dear fellow, no killing is intended. At least no killing of American agents. We want no trouble with your country. All we intend is to hold you until you can no longer interfere with important events that are about to transpire here in Baja. After that you'll be quite free to go." He stopped. I didn't say anything. He went on: "François had to run your girl off the road in her little car; but he says there is no serious or permanent damage, at least not to the girl—at the worst, he says, a slight concussion and a broken collarbone. He is a very skillful driver; I am sure he picked his spot carefully. He always does."

"Good for François," I said. "Sit down and take a load off your drama, Colonel Huntington."

He smiled thinly. "I was wondering if you knew me. We almost met once, didn't we, Mr. Helm?" He glanced down. "I said that no killing is *intended*. People have been killed unintentionally when they brandished firearms in an indiscriminate manner. I mention this, you understand, just in case that should be a revolver you're holding under the table. I should also point out that your governmental bodyguard outside is sleeping soundly; my man Simi is very good with sentries and guards. There are more of my men outside. If you start shooting, you will never get out of here alive."

"If it comes to shooting," I said, "neither will you, Colonel."

"In that case, with no one to control them, my grieving men will undoubtedly kill the girl."

I said, "Now that we've growled at each other adequately, all we have to do is pee on the nearest telephone pole and the amenities will be taken care of. Suppose we dispense with the menace and get to the point."

He hesitated, and pulled out the chair facing me, and seated himself. "I merely wished to make the situation perfectly clear, old chap."

"Well, you didn't succeed," I said. "You forgot the main thing. What's your beef?"

He frowned. "What do you mean?"

"What am I doing that you object to, Colonel?" I asked. "Why does my presence in Baja disturb you so much that you have to disable my escort, capture my assistant, and threaten me with kidnaping and death? What am I doing that's got you all worked up?"

"Do you need to ask?"

"I wouldn't ask if I didn't need to."

He made a sharp little gesture. "Let's not play games, Helm. Do you think I have forgotten General Jorge Santos? You remember Santos, I'm certain—the would-be dictator who called himself El Fuerte, down in Costa Verde—well, let's call it Costa Verde, since that was the code you people used for it, I believe. Operation Costa Verde. I was in line for some very profitable employment down there, until you shot Santos out from under me; a very fine shot, I understand, over five hundred meters. I offer my congratulations, a few years late. But once is enough, my dear fellow. I don't intend to lose any more generals, or jobs, on your account. When I heard you were coming and why—"

"Hold everything!" I said. "Let me get this straight. Are you rounding me up, and my lady helper, because you think we've got designs on the life of your precious and irreplaceable General Díaz?"

"What else?" he asked, surprised. "That's what our informants tell us, and it checks with everything we know about you, old chap. You're an expert at homicide. Well, we're all experts at homicide here, but your particular specialty, and that of your attractive little colleague, is disposing of them singly instead of in bulk, so to speak. What other target could you, or the United States government, have down here in Baja except that potential disturber of the precarious peace of the Americas, General Hernando Díaz? Obviously, you have been sent to do to Díaz precisely what you did to Santos some years back, for much the same reasons. Just as then, you have the backing of the government in power, which has assigned a man to protect you until you can get your work done. Our information is that your Mexican government associates have even supplied you with a very similar long-range rifle for the job."

"Well, I don't consider a light sporting .270 very similar to a heavy, target-type .300 Magnum, but I suppose that's a matter of opinion." I looked at him bleakly. At some time in the past, a bullet had cut a groove at the angle of his jaw; a couple of inches to the side and it would have taken off half his head and I'd never have met him. Well, there would have been another one sitting there, probably, just as coldly professional. The woods are full of them. "Who's in charge here?" I asked at last.

"Why, I am, old chap."

I shook my head irritably. "Cut it out. You know what I mean. We're both hired hands. I take orders from a guy in Washington. You're presumably working for the so-called Sanctuary Corporation. Well, who's calling the shots for them locally? Who gives you your instructions?"

He hesitated. "I see no reason to—"

"There's every reason," I said. "You boys are making a

very bad mistake. I want to talk with the man at the top, and I don't mean any turncoat, two-bit figurehead generals or, begging your pardon, any hireling colonels either. This high-powered international outfit of yours is bound to have at least one real representative here with authority to act for it. Can you take me to him?"

His sun-bleached blue eyes studied me for a long moment. "I've read the dossier," he said, slowly. "You have a reputation for trickery—"

"No tricks," I said. "Let's put all the cards on the table, Colonel. You can kill me, sure, or your men can; but you can't take me alive if I don't want to be taken alive. And if I force you to shoot it out with me in this room, there'll be a real bloodbath, with innocent Yankee fishermen dying all over the place. Publicity galore, just what your revolution doesn't need right now. Is that a fair statement of the situation? Please notice, I'm not even trading on the fact that the first one to die will be you. I'm taking for granted that we're all brave as lions around here, and death doesn't scare us a bit. But we're not here to die, either of us, are we? We've both got jobs to do. I'd like a chance to demonstrate that those jobs are not as incompatible as you seem to think, but I want to do my talking to somebody with real clout. Okay?"

After I'd finished making my speech, it occurred to me that it was just a variation of the gaudy gambit I'd used on Andrew Euler, back at the border—the bloody-massacre ploy, you might call it. Well, why change a winning game? I like living, and the only way you keep living in this business is to make damned sure nobody ever gets the notion you're scared of dying; that brings them down on you like vultures zeroing in on a sick steer. The man across the table was regarding me suspiciously.

"Are you trying to tell me that you're not here after Díaz?"

"No," I said. "I'm not trying to tell you anything, Colonel Huntington. It would be a waste of time, wouldn't it?

Even if I convinced you, I'd still have to go through the whole routine with somebody else, wouldn't I? All I'll say to you is that you're making a mistake, and it could turn out to be a very serious mistake for you, if you don't let me talk with the man on top."

He said, "If you're trying to be clever—"

I said, "Goddamn it, how did you ever manage to win any wars if you can't make up your cotton-picking mind? Put your hand under the table. . . . Come on, come on, reach down there! Have you got it? One Smith and Wesson loaded with five. Next, one Colt loaded with six. That's eleven people who don't die tonight. Now the knife. Okay, Colonel. Your move. . . ."

nineteen ....

There were four of us in the big Mercedes. The little man with the beret, whom Huntington had called François, had the wheel. Beside him was the black man referred to as Simi—presumably a nickname since that was an African word for knife, if I remembered my safari novels correctly. The colonel and I shared the luxurious rear seat.

"Very well, François, let's pay a visit to *Monsieur Bleu*," Huntington said. As the car started up smoothly, he laughed. "These bloody amateur revolutionaries and their bloody secret corporations! *Monsieuir* Bleu. *Señor Rojo. Herr* Braun. Mr. Green. I fancy it makes them feel clever and conspiratorial, but if they don't want to be recognized by the lower orders they should wear masks. Even we illiterate, plebeian mercenaries occasionally glance at the photographs of the wealthy and beautiful in the illustrated public press."

"The whole spectrum, eh?" I said.

"Like a bloody rainbow, old chap. But you'll meet only

the blue *Monsieur* tonight. How's your command of the French language?"

"Lousy."

Huntington sighed. "Then I'll have to translate, I fear. *Monsieur* does not condescend to comprehend the lousy French. You know how Frenchmen are about their language, With a Spaniard or Mexican, if you know three words of Spanish and make a determined effort to use them, those lovely people will do everything in their power to teach you the rest of the dictionary, but the bloody French. . . . Yes, I mean you, François. You've been correcting my pronunciation ever since we met, you Gallic monkey. Is this as fast as this Hun machine will operate?" The driver, apparently unperturbed, said something over his shoulder in French. "Never mind them," said Huntington. "They know where to come. Let us proceed to our destination with some celerity, *s'il vous plaît.*" The limousine surged ahead, and the lights in the rearview mirror, visible from my position, diminished in size and, eventually, vanished. Two of them were lights that should have been familiar to me, since they were the headlights of my own carryall; except that I'd never made a study of it from outside with the lights on. It was serving as an ambulance, at Huntington's suggestion. He'd thought Norma would have a more comfortable ride on a purloined hotel mattress in the rear of the big truck-stationwagon than trying to sit up in a sedan.

It was a point in his favor, as was the fact that, unlike some other men I'd met under similar circumstances, he'd seen no need to push me around after he had me disarmed. He had not, however, let me talk with Norma. I'd only caught a glimpse of her sagging between two men, small and pale and disheveled, as we were escorted to the cars. Keeping us separate made sense, of course. That way we couldn't compare notes and agree on the story we were going to tell.

"Militarily speaking, this operation should be a piece of cake," Huntington said abruptly after we'd driven for a while in silence. "In case you were wondering about the feasibility of our revolutionary project, old chap. It may seem like a fairly ambitious undertaking; but the fact is that the Mexicans are being kept very busy over in the Sierra Madre, on the mainland. They are not making their internal difficulties public, but when I drove through there to assess the situation recently, I found military checkpoints everywhere. I even spotted one of their crack Commando units in the area—copied from your Green Berets, I believe—some chaps I was hoping not to have to deal with here. It appears that my hope will be fulfilled—"

He stopped as the car lurched violently, braking hard. The headlights showed a battered van with California plates on the road ahead—there are more Californians on the Baja roads than there are Bajans—and it had moved over deliberately to block us as we tried to pass. The colonel reached down and brought up a submachine gun that had been reposing between his feet. He glanced at me.

"What do you think, old chap? An ambush, perhaps?"

"Maybe," I said. "Or just some Yankee drunks being funny, ha-ha. I'm not expecting a rescue, if that's what you mean."

"Would you say so if you were?"

I said, "You didn't take my weapons, *amigo*. I gave them to you, remember?"

"That wouldn't prevent some of your official Mexican friends from coming to your assistance, although that hardly looks like the sort of vehicle they'd use. Let's see what they have in mind," He reached out and tapped François on the head, speaking softly: "I thought you were supposed to be a driver, little man. What do you need to pass that heap of rusty metal, a military tank?"

The narrow shoulders of the man behind the wheel rose and fell in an expressive shrug. The Mercedes moved up once more, flashing its headlights for permission to pass, in the European manner. The swaying truck ahead, its windows blocked with luggage and camping gear, moved once more into the center of the road. I felt fairly helpless. If Ramón had been alerted and was trying to interfere, he could very well get me killed, and if it was just some crazy American kids on a camping trip, or some other kind of a trip, well, it would be a hell of a stupid way to get smashed up. . . .

The colonel sat quite still beside me, the chopper on his knees. François probed to one side and the other, trying to feint the driver ahead out of position; then the Frenchman found a hole and the limousine shot forward, horn blaring. As we passed, I caught a glimpse of two young men and a girl in the van, the girl in the middle, holding a can of beer where the driver could reach it when he was not too busy driving.

Huntington drew a long, restrained breath as we pulled away. "I have a revolution to arrange," he said. "I have to deal with temperamental millionaires, incompetent generals, crazy ships' captains, untrained troops, unreliable suppliers, and a mysterious marksman with a big rifle; and what happens? Beer-swilling hippies try to play games with me on the public—"

He stopped, as headlights moved up alongside. In spite of our considerable speed, the battered van with the U.S. plates was trying to pass us. As the cab of the truck came abreast of our rear windows, the male passenger reached out and made the standard obscene gesture with his finger, quite visible in the kickback of the headlights. Beyond him, I could see the girl and the driver laughing uproariously. . . .

"I believe," said the colonel calmly, "that we have suffered quite enough of that. Attend to it, François, please."

The Mercedes increased speed. The truck stopped gaining and hung level with our rear door. Slowly, inexorably, the long limousine started to move over. I saw the expression on the face at the window of the van's cab change from malicious elation to incredulity and fear. The truck's horn bleated feebly in protest. The driver braked hard, trying to get out from under, but he was too late. He had no road left to drive on; it was full of Mercedes. I saw the headlights dip as the vehicle went off into the ditch. François pulled the limousine around a sudden curve, the steel-belted radials clawing for traction. Fortunately there was no other traffic on the road at this time of night.

"Turn around," the colonel said. "I think we're obliged to finish the lesson, now that we have started it."

He sat silent beside me as the car was turned and sent back to the spot. The occupants of the van had been lucky. It was fairly precipitous country in spots, but they had chosen to do their Mercedes-baiting on a level stretch. They'd simply bounced out across the wide, shallow, roadside ditch and brought up, not too hard, against one of the volcanic boulders that dotted the countryside here. When we stopped above them, the two men were assisting the girl out of the van. She'd apparently been thrown against the windshield. There was considerable blood, visible even in the dark. One of the men started towards us, to ask for assistance, I suppose, and then checked himself as he recognized the distinctive car.

"Simi," Huntington said, "That's the fellow, I do believe, the one with the darker beard. You saw the gesture. I suggest you take steps to prevent a recurrence, if you know what I mean. Then bring me the driver."

The black man got out deliberately, and moved down there. At the last moment, the dark-bearded youth tried to run, but he was still shaky from the accident, and Simi had no trouble catching him and bringing him down. There was a brief struggle. A moment later, a knife gleamed in the darkness, and there were a couple of screams of pain followed by some whimpering sobs. The other two, who had started that way, perhaps with some intention of helping, had stopped. The girl put her hands to her bloody face. She remained standing there as Simi brought the second youth to the car.

"Here is the finger," the black man said to Huntington. "He will not make that gesture again, not with that hand, sir."

"Put it into the pocket of his friend here." The colonel leaned towards the window. "You."

The driver of the van was staring with horror at the dripping object the black man was stuffing into the pocket of his grimy denim shirt.

"Are you people crazy?" he cried wildly. "What the hell do you think—"

"Be quiet," Huntington said. "You're a drunken and objectionable young fool. Let's probe the depths of your stupidity. Describe this car."

The youth licked his lips and glanced at the knife in Simi's hand. "Why . . . why it's a Mercedes, I forget the exact model. . . ."

"Wrong answer." The colonel lifted his submachine gun and laid the muzzle on the car's windowsill. "One more chance. Describe the car."

"Oh." The boy stared at the weapon, wide-eyed. After a long moment, he said breathlessly, "Why, it's a big American car, sir, I think a Cadillac or Lincoln—"

"That's better, much better. Now describe the man who just maimed your friend with a knife."

"He was black. . . ." He saw the chopper move slightly, and gulped. "No, no, please don't. . . . I mean, I'm sorry, what man? What knife? The whole thing was my fault, I tried to pass where I shouldn't have and we went off the road and Jerry put his hand through the windshield and the broken glass. . . ." He stopped, out of breath.

"I hope you have a very good memory," Colonel Huntington said. "I hope you and your friends recall the incident precisely as you have just described it. I wouldn't want to have to send somebody back to correct the official record because one of you had made an error in reporting this unfortunate accident. . . . Oh, one more thing."

"Yes, sir."

"In the future, when a faster car wishes to pass, you'll move over politely and let it by, won't you, my dear young fellow?"

"Y-yes, sir."

"As for your friend, since apparently he has no better uses for his finger, he's just as well off without it, isn't he? You might suggest to him that if he nevertheless persists in being rude to passing travelers, it's quite possible to find something else to cut off him, don't you know?"

We drove away in silence. I couldn't help thinking it had been pretty stupid behavior for a pro, risking trouble with the authorities for a matter of little importance. On the other hand, it had given me a warning insight into the character of the pale-eyed individual beside me, who'd go to the trouble of stealing a mattress for an injured girl, to be sure, but who was also capable of retaliating savagely for a very minor insult and inconvenience.

I heard him chuckle in the darkness. "You're wondering what all that was in aid of, aren't you?"

"More or less," I said cautiously.

He laughed again, but when he spoke his voice was serious: "Helm, we've created a world that's a perfect environment for toughs and outlaws. They feel they can do anything they please, absolutely anything, because the peaceful citizen has been disarmed and taught never to resist, no matter what happens. To redress the balance slightly, I feel it my duty now and then to demonstrate that there are a few chaps around who will strike back if sufficiently provoked."

I grinned. "Jeez," I said, "the thinking man's soldier of fortune, no less."

I heard him laugh once more, but I think I'd hurt his feelings, and we rode the rest of the way without speaking. Presently, a few road signs and some scattered lights off to the left indicated that we were passing—bypassing, rather—the town of Loreto. At last the Mercedes turned off the paved highway onto a track almost as bad as the one that had led me to Laguna de la Muerte that morning. The little man at the wheel coaxed the limousine skillfully through the rough going, however, and brought it to a stop on a low bluff overlooking a small bay of the Gulf of California. A shadowy shape out there indicated a sizable motor yacht riding at anchor in the center of the bay.

François flashed the headlights in a signal. Almost instantly we heard the sound of an outboard motor and saw a small boat heading towards us. A few minutes later the colonel and I were climbing aboard the mother ship, a fairly impressive craft. A trawler is a rugged fishing vessel designed to carry big loads of fish and lots of gear through heavy seas. A trawler yacht is something else again. It retains to some extent the husky, seaworthy outward appearance of the working craft from which it is derived, because that's what sells boats these days when the docks are full of instant Magellans with fast checkbooks; but it's actually just another luxury bucket under the camouflage. I was willing to bet that no fish had ever come aboard the *Esperanza* (Acapulco) unless it was solidly frozen or at least very carefully wrapped so it wouldn't drip on the pretty teak deck.

The well-lighted, heavily curtained main cabin was a symphony of elaborate paneling and shiny parquet flooring. There was a rug that had never felt the tread of a heavy seaboot, a shiny cocktail table never scratched by anything so crude and useful as a sextant, and beautifully upholstered chairs that had never supported weary seamen in dripping oilskins, or whatever passes for oilskins these days. The slender man waiting for us there was very handsome and elegant, in full yachting regalia, with smooth dark hair and a penciled little moustache; but when the light hit him right it was clear he wasn't as young as he'd like you to think. I'd never seen him before or his photograph. Perhaps, unlike the colonel, I didn't pay enough attention to the doings of the beautiful rich. He spoke to us, as I had been warned, in French.

"*Monsieur* Bleu wants to know why I am bothering him with you," Huntington said. "Why *am* I bothering him with you, old chap?"

"To keep your General Díaz from being assassinated by a professional automatic weapons expert named Ernemann," I said.

twenty ••••••••••••••••••••••••••••

The cabin serving as my detention cell was way up forward in the boat and obviously had been designed as quarters for a couple of crewmen. White-painted and unadorned, it wasn't fancy enough for guests. It had two berths, one above the other, a small washbasin, and a little head—nautical for john—hidden under a padded seat. The whole thing wasn't much bigger than a train compartment. The single porthole wasn't large enough to let a cat escape, even if it could be opened, which I doubted. This was a truly modern yacht; and it seemed that truly modern yachtsmen don't go boating to expose themselves to fresh sea air—at least all ventilation here was by air-conditioning.

I washed at the little sink. *Monsieur* Bleu had fancied himself as a latter-day inquisitor. Unlike his military adviser, he enjoyed slapping people around. As torture, it had been childish. If I'd had some secrets I wanted to preserve, I'd hardly have yielded them for a few slaps in the face. The *Monsieur's* forehand had actually been quite bearable. However, I'd had a little trouble with his backhand, since he was wearing a large signet ring. . . .

Some time later, voices sounded in the passage outside. The door opened, and Norma stumbled in, supported by a man who released her, once she'd passed the doorway, and let her fall into my arms. I saw that her right arm was supported by an impromptu sling—somebody's big blue bandana—and her face was cut and bleeding just like mine. That damned ring was really getting a workout. It occurred to me that there had been a lot of blood shed tonight for very little. I'd managed to kill two men the previous morning without making half the mess.

I eased my burden gently onto the seat covering the seagoing plumbing. "How goes it, Chicana?" I asked.

Her head came up sharply. "I told you not to call me—" She stopped when I laughed.

"I thought that would snap you out of it," I said. "What's the matter with the arm?"

"I think it's just the collarbone," she said. "I felt something go snap in there when the Datsun hit. I also cracked my head a moment later, and I've got the world's biggest headache, and that elegant old bastard with the nautical brass buttons and the dyed hair didn't make it any better." She hesitated. "I told him. There wasn't any reason to be heroic, was there?"

"Not any," I said. "Quite the contrary. What did you tell him?"

"About Ernemann, mostly. What little I knew."

"Good," I said. "Now he's heard the same story from two sources. Now maybe he'll warm up the fancy electronics on this glamor-bucket and check it out with his fancy international intelligence system and learn it's the truth. Well, that'll take some hours. Let's clean you up and put you to bed while we wait—"

"Matt."

"What?"

She was looking up at me in an odd way. "You did send me north to keep me out of danger, didn't you?"

I hesitated, and said, "Why risk trained manpower for nothing? Okay, womanpower. And the subject of Euler does require some research—"

She said, "Yes, that's why I went. You were very persuasive, even though I knew what you had at the back of your mind. But that's enough of that. Maybe we're not supposed to be strong, silent heroes, but we're not supposed to be sentimental jerks, either."

I frowned. "I don't understand—"

"Stop it!" she snapped. "You know perfectly well what I mean. I'm not in very good escaping condition at the moment, if you've got it in mind to break out of here somehow. And on the other hand, if you're planning to talk your way out, well, it's not very likely they'll let me go with you, is it? I don't know exactly how the situation stands, but if they do let you go it's because they want something from you. And in that case, it's inevitable that they'll hold me here as a hostage for your good behavior —in fact, that's probably why they grabbed me in the first place. Am I right?"

I said, "Hold still while I mop you off a little. Let's not borrow trouble—"

"Don't give me that big strong masculine runaround, damn you!" she said angrily. "I want you to remember that we don't play the hostage game in this outfit. I don't want to lie here after you're gone, wondering if maybe you're letting yourself be blackmailed into doing something, or not doing it, because of anything that might happen to me. Maybe I'm flattering myself, maybe you wouldn't consider it, but I want to make damned sure you don't. Men get funny romantic notions about girls to whom they've made love, if you want to use the word to describe our Mexico City quickie. Well, don't you get any funny notions about me, hear? I'm a pro, Buster, and this

is my assignment as well as yours. . . . What I mean is, if
you screw up *our* mission just to save the little Spanish-
American cutie's precious minority-type life, I'll cut my
damn throat to spite you. You'll save nothing. That's a
promise."

I looked down at her respectfully for a moment. Then I
tipped her chin up and kissed her lightly on the mouth.
"Not to worry, Virginia Dominguez," I said. "Rest assured that your welfare will be the very smallest of my
worries. Okay?"

They came for me towards morning. There were two of
them, husky Mexicans in white ship's uniforms; and they
were cautious about opening the door. One had a pistol.

"Come," said the nearest one, the unarmed one.

"The señorita?" I asked.

"The señorita, she stays."

I slid off the top bunk and winked at Norma and went
out past them, hearing the door being closed and locked
behind me. They nudged me along to the main cabin,
where my host was having brandy out of a big, balloon-
shaped glass, which he warmed tenderly with both hands.
It seemed early in the morning for brandy, but maybe I
was looking at it from the wrong point of view. Maybe I
should have been considering it as just pleasantly late at
night. Colonel Peter Huntington stood at one of the big
curtained windows. There was a brandy snifter in his
hand, also, but he wasn't making quite as big a produc-
tion of bringing it up to the proper scientific temperature.

"Who's Soo?" he asked.

"Who's who?"

I'd forgotten my host, the Gallic Torquemada. He reminded me of his presence by setting aside his drink,
stepping forward, and fetching me a sharp crack across
the cheek that made my eyes water. Forehand, fortunately. He spoke sharply to Huntington.

"Monsieur Bleu says this is no time for levity, old chap. Be so good as to answer the question. A gentleman named Soo. Identity, please?"

Actually, I'd been stalling for time to pull my thoughts together. The name was familiar, of course. Mac had made a big point of dragging in a reference to the Chinaman during one of our telephone conversations. It had obviously been a warning, but there had been no further suggestions of Oriental involvement, so it had almost slipped my mind.

"To be accurate," I said, "the gentleman is not named Soo. The real name is something like High Fat or Low Duck; we've got it in the dossier somewhere. We don't use it because he doesn't, at least not on this continent. He calls himself Mr. Soo. We call him that, or the Chinaman. The term is not intended to be flattering."

I knew the real name, but I saw no reason to volunteer it. Let them pry it out of me. But they didn't bother.

"A Red Chinese agent?" Huntington asked.

"Correct."

"You've had dealings with him?"

"It depends on what you mean by dealings," I said carefully. "I've come up against him a number of times, three to be exact."

"Who won?"

"Well, we're both still alive, at least he was the last time I heard. So I guess neither of us has really *won*, yet. On points, I think I'm a bit ahead."

"Why didn't you tell us this earlier?"

I started to speak and checked myself. I'd been about to say that I hadn't mentioned it because it hadn't occurred to me, because I'd had only a hint of Soo's involvement, and I still had no idea how a Chinese agent figured in a Mexican revolution. However, just as it isn't smart to volunteer too much information, it's poor technique to display too much ignorance, if only because people will generally refuse to believe that you're that dumb even if you are.

I said, "Maybe I didn't think it was any of your damned business."

That got me a backhand from my host even before it was translated, showing how much he really needed a translator. He fired some crackling French at the colonel.

"*Monsieur* Bleu says that you have wasted most of a night by withholding the information from us. If you'd let us know the truth at once, things could have been settled much more quickly."

Frankly, I didn't know what truth he was talking about. Obviously, these people had found a piece of the puzzle I hadn't been privileged to see—Soo, for God's sake!—and just as obviously it wasn't strategic or diplomatic for me to ask how it fit.

"Sorry," I said. "I figured it was a personal matter."

Strangely, that seemed to make sense to Huntington, even though it made none to me.

"Your story about this man Ernemann has been confirmed," he said. "We find your motive for wishing to eliminate him quite convincing. I apologize for the misunderstanding, old chap. It seems that we're fighting in the same army for a change, at least temporarily."

I dabbed with my handkerchief at a bleeding lip that had encountered the family crest of the Bleus. I said sourly, "It is a great privilege, Colonel."

"There's only one thing we haven't been able to determine," he said. "Who hired this professional killer to dispose of Díaz?"

I said, "We're not quite sure of that, either. One theory, for what it's worth, is that Ernemann was hired by Mrs. Clarissa O'Hearn, who then arranged to ride along with me so she could take me out of action if I started getting close enough to interfere."

"Mrs. O'Hearn?" He was startled. "You mean, Oscar's wife—"

"Your liaison man isn't really God's gift to matrimony, Colonel. The lady with whom he lives—well, when he's home—hates his guts. Maybe even enough to hire somebody to louse up his pet revolution so she can laugh in his face."

"Maybe? You're not certain?"

"No, I'm not," I said. "It's just one theory, and I'm not very fond of it myself. I don't find the motive convincing, after spending some time with the lady."

"Do you have an alternative to suggest?"

I shook my head. "My Mexican friend, Solana-Ruiz, seems to figure it's cut and dried, like any cop who's found a plausible solution to a case. He's got a lot of evidence, but I'm not sold, so if you have any suggestions—"

Huntington hesitated, and said, "Well, come to think of it, there is a certain group down here in Baja that would like to see us fail—apart from the loyal Mexicans, I mean. There is already a large number of foreigners settled here, don't you know, mostly Americans. They are quite satisfied with the status quo. They've complied with the Mexican requirements, they don't want the rules changed, they don't want the waters muddied by any kind of violent intervention. They feel they discovered this picturesque, undeveloped paradise for themselves, and they have no desire to see it taken over by an organization of wealthy refugees from civilization—an organization that, even if successful, could give them nothing they don't already have, and would probably favor its own members over the people already on the ground."

Monsieur Bleu cleared his throat for attention. He spoke contemptuously and at length. When he was through, I looked to Huntington for the translation.

The colonel said, *"Monsieur* Bleu says the great Sanctuary Corporation can't be expected to consider the individual problems of every little Yankee squatter already here. He says some efforts were made, early on, to approach certain leading American residents of Baja, but they weren't interested so let them take the consequences."

"I see," I said. "What it amounts to is that you've got nothing much to offer these emigrants from the U.S. if you succeed. On the other hand, if you fail, you'll make all foreigners so unpopular in Mexico that they'll probably have to pack up and leave, losing everything they've built here. It's an interesting angle. I hadn't thought of it. I suppose these characters aren't exactly impoverished."

"Some of them are quite wealthy, I believe."

"So if one of them came up with a sound plan for stopping your takeover, Colonel, he might be able to finance it—say the fee of a guy named Ernemann—by passing the hat among his well-heeled *Americano* friends and neighbors. Have you any indications that they're up to something like that?"

"Not really," Huntington said, "Anyway, the question of responsibility is rather academic, old chap. The fact is that this fellow Ernemann is among us and something must be done about him immediately. He's been reported in La Paz, as you said. He's apparently heading south towards Cabo San Lucas. I don't believe it's a coincidence that General Díaz is scheduled for some important conferences in the area. The general must make an appearance. We need the support of the people he is to meet. We can't recall him; we can't even warn him to be careful. Unfortunately, he's one of these very virile Mexican chaps—what is the word they use so frequently?"

"Macho?"

"Righto. To ask our *macho* general to lie low because there's danger would be to question his courage, don't you know? He's the kind of stupid poseur who fears nothing so much as having somebody think him afraid. I've managed to slip a bodyguard onto the plane under the guise of adjutant and personal secretary to his military highness, but if I were to warn Díaz directly, he'd simply make a point of strutting around in the open like a fat peacock to prove how brave he is." Huntington sighed. "It's always the way, old chap. One can deal with the enemy; it's the friends who defeat one, rather."

"Oh, rather," I said.

He smiled thinly. "Since it's practically impossible to protect the fool, I'd like to eliminate the danger to him—this Ernemann—as quickly as possible."

"Oh, righto," I said. "Just what I was about to do when I was so rudely delayed, old chap."

He laughed shortly. "To be sure. I apologize again for the misunderstanding. Before you leave, I'll brief you on Díaz's itinerary; then you'll be taken to your vehicle on shore. Your rifle and ammunition have not been touched. Your money and your other weapons will, of course, be returned. Any assistance we can give, you have only to ask for. Satisfactory?"

"It's a deal," I said.

There was a barrage of rapid-fire French from the handsome elderly gent with the brass-buttoned blazer and the big signet ring. Colonel Huntington sighed, and said rather reluctantly, *"Monsieur* Bleu has reminded me of one detail I forgot to mention. The young lady."

It wasn't hard to guess what was coming. I gave Norma a passing grade in clairvoyance.

"What," I asked, "about the young lady?"

"Monsieur Bleu says—I do regret this, my dear fellow, but it's a necessary precaution—*Monsieur* Bleu says that the girl's life and that of General Hernando Díaz are now very closely linked. Inextricably intertwined, you might say. As long as you keep Díaz alive, you keep your pretty agent alive. If Díaz dies, she dies. Understood?"

I drew a long breath, and said, "I thought you folks didn't want to antagonize the U.S. by killing any American agents."

The colonel hesitated. It was the Frenchman who answered, taking my arm and swinging me around to face him. He said harshly, in perfectly clear and only slightly accented English: "If we do not have the figurehead general, we do not have the revolution. If we do not have the revolution, what does it matter whom we antagonize? *Comprenez-vous?*"

I comprehended, all right.

twenty-one ....

The track leading back to the main highway that had seemed kind of tricky and risky in Huntington's low-slung limousine was, of course, no problem at all in my high-riding four-wheel-drive truck. I felt strange, however, driving it across the rugged landscape all alone. It had been a real togetherness trip to date. I wondered where Clarissa was being held and how she was bearing up in captivity. I didn't wonder about Norma. I knew where she was being held, and I knew she was bearing up all right because that was what she was paid for. I decided it was better not to think too much about Norma and what she was paid for, under the circumstances.

I stopped after a couple of miles, as the road emerged on a reasonably level plain suitable for a testing project I had in mind. The sun was almost up; there was light enough to see. Whoever had driven the ambulance down from Mulege with Norma lying in the rear had left a couple of empty Mexican beer cans on the floor. I picked them up, got out, paced off two hundred yards, and set them on a little rocky ridge out there. Hiking back, I slipped the .270 from its cheap plastic case, loaded it with two cartridges, and took a firm rest with my elbows on the hood of the carryall. You don't want to let the barrel touch anything, and even the wooden forearm shouldn't rest against anything too hard and unyielding. There's a lot of whip when a high-powered rifle is fired. Anything that disturbs the natural barrel vibrations will throw the bullet off target.

It was a calm morning; no windage estimates were required. At my first shot, the left-hand can went spinning away; the second shot took care of the right-hand one. I wished I'd had money riding on those shots; they were actually a little better than they should have been. I hoped I could do as well when it really counted. Anyway, Colonel Peter Huntington was a truthful man, at least sometimes, and nobody'd monkeyed with my rifle—but it isn't something I like to take anybody's word for when I've got a job to do.

I wiped off the piece with my handkerchief. It wasn't the most beautiful firearm in the world—a second-hand Remington with the kind of bargain-basement checkering that's crudely stamped into the wood of the stock instead of being neatly cut by hand or machine—but it shot all right, which was what mattered. I slipped the gun back into the case and zippered it up, knowing that I was stalling. I was trying to make up my mind about some things I had learned.

Ernemann himself didn't worry me too much. There's always a small nagging doubt, of course, when you're going up against a good pro—this could be the time you get unlucky, or simply meet a better man—but I had a reliable, accurate rifle, and the information I'd received about General Díaz's schedule had suggested a fairly promising plan based on the fact that the small, unfenced, and scantily manned airstrips associated with many of the luxury hotels in Baja are practically made for assassination purposes. I couldn't see Ernemann, the chopper expert, passing up a lovely, open field of fire like that to do his work under more cramped and unfavorable circumstances elsewhere. All I had to do was lure him to the right place and be there ahead of him.

No, Ernemann was a straightforward problem of the kind I was trained to solve. It was the other pieces of the puzzle that had me slightly baffled—Mr. Soo, for instance —but I couldn't spend any more time brooding about them now. I got back into the truck. Soon I was heading south down the main highway at a moderate clip. For a while, it seemed as if I was being followed discreetly at a considerable distance, but eventually the car behind disappeared. I was beginning to wonder if I'd been imagining things when I saw the blocky shape of Ramón's big Japanese boondocks buggy coming up fast astern. There were two people visible inside. I slowed down. The Toyota drove past and ducked off the road and stopped. I swung down there and pulled up behind it. Ramón got out and came back to where I was parked and got into the carryall beside me.

"We can talk as we drive," he said. "Go on. Amado will follow."

"How is my friend Amado?" I asked, sending the carryall back onto the pavement. "He wasn't a hell of a lot of help. The black man took him like Grant took Richmond."

"Grant? Richmond?" Apparently they didn't teach much U.S. Civil War history in Mexican schools, or he'd forgotten what little he'd learned. "Amado is all right," Ramón went on, when I didn't bother to explain. "He has a very hard head."

"Good for Amado," I said. "How'd you pick me up so fast?"

"Oh, we've been keeping an eye on the Marquis de Beaupré and his yacht, particularly since we discovered that you were missing," Ramón said. "Amado described the people involved, when he returned to consciousness, so we knew with whom we were dealing. My man spotted you driving away just now and followed a little way to make certain you were heading south, meanwhile calling me on the two-way radio. I was waiting back in Loreto. You gave me quite a chase."

I saw no need to apologize. "So the Frenchman is a marquis. I thought they'd stopped making them."

"Raoul Archambeau, Marquis de Beaupré. Not a pleasant man but a very wealthy one. He is also supposed to be brilliant in a financial way."

"The yacht wasn't French. The *Esperanza,* out of Acapulco."

"She belongs to a certain *Señor* Ramirez—*Señor* Rojo, as he is called by his associates in the Sanctuary Corporation." When I glanced at him sharply, Ramón grinned. "Oh, yes, we know all about the powerful, secret, international corporation. We know about its hired military genius. We know about the network of dissidents established all over South Baja, now being briefed and encouraged by General Díaz personally for the great day of liberation soon to come. We know about the shock troops being trained in the desert, and the supply ships moving towards our coasts, loaded with expensive military hardware." His grin had faded. His voice was harsh. "We know a great deal, *amigo,* but we can do very little. As I have already told you, we are very busy elsewhere."

I made a sympathetic sound. "You've got a problem, all right."

"With a handful of men and a few pesos," he said, "I am asked to perform a miracle; and it must not only be a miracle, it must be a silent and invisible miracle." He went on without waiting for my comment: "As for finding you, it seemed likely that you would be taken to the yacht, particularly after we picked up a trio of damaged California hippies who'd had an encounter with a big

Mercedes heading that way. The description of one of the passengers, a very sinister-appearing tall *hombre,* reminded me a little, just a little, of you."

"It would have been nice if you'd sent a boarding party," I said, feeling my cut lip.

"What, interfere with the yacht of the powerful *Señor* Ramirez, chartered for a pleasure cruise to that influential French financier, the fabulously wealthy Marquis de Beaupré? You must be mad, friend Matthew, to expect such reckless and illegal actions of a poor little underpaid Mexican government clerk."

I grinned. "So you got the kids in the van to talk. Frankly, although they'd asked for it, I thought it was kind of dumb of Colonel Huntington to take time out from his work to teach them manners. However, he threw a pretty good scare into them to keep them quiet."

Ramón said, "I throw a pretty good scare myself, *amigo.*"

"Sure you do," I said. "Sometimes you even scare me. Like when you assign one lone man to save me from a whole revolutionary army—without even a word of warning to me."

There was a little silence. The car ran on smoothly. The sun was up now, throwing our long shadow ahead of us on the two-lane blacktop road. At the moment we were heading west, inland, away from the Gulf of California; that highway just zig-zags back and forth between one shore of the Baja peninsula to the other.

"You have my apologies," Ramón said at last, reluctantly. Admitting error doesn't come easy below the border, or anywhere else, I guess. "I miscalculated. I knew they were in the neighborhood, but I could see no reason why they should have business with you, so there seemed to be no reason to tell you." He hesitated. "How did you persuade them to let you go?"

"They were operating under a misapprehension," I

said. "I managed to clear it up, and convince them that our interests were identical."

"Tell me."

I told him. It took a little while.

"I see," Ramón said at last. "So now you *must* stop Ernemann or your female agent dies."

I hadn't been too specific about where Norma had been keeping herself, and why she'd been staying under cover, and he hadn't asked for details.

I shrugged. "Hell, I was going to stop him anyway. That's what I'm here for, isn't it?"

"Yes, of course," Ramon said. "And you think you can lure him to this one particular airstrip at the Hotel Cabo San Lucas?"

"The way to catch a tiger, I'm told, is to stake out a fat bullock for bait. I think Ernemann will come to a fat bullock named Díaz. Colonel Huntington is making arrangements for an information leak; plenty of people will soon know that Díaz and his entourage will be landing there tomorrow morning according to plan."

Ramón said, "He is very trusting, this colonel. He is putting his revolution—the man who represents it, at least —entirely into your hands."

"Trusting, hell," I said. "I told you, he's got Norma. I've got no choice, and the fact of the matter is, as I said, our interests are identical. He's got to take some risk to get rid of Ernemann, and I was sent down here to take care of just that. Even if I was willing to let the girl be killed, why should I double-cross him? What have I got to gain?"

"Very well," Ramón said. He glanced at the dashboard. "But if you plan to drive all the way to Cabo San Lucas today you had better get some gas. There's a little town called Ciudad Constitucion ahead. . . ."

It took a while to tank up, since the single station in the town was crowded and we had to wait in line. I paid the bill, which was sizable; it was a big tank, and the better grade of Mexican gas costs around three pesos a liter these days, which works out to very close to a buck a gallon. When I returned to the carryall, Ramon was just climbing back into the copilot's seat.

"Wait for Amado," he said. "I sent him across the street for some beer."

"I hope you had him get some for me."

"Of course, *amigo.*"

Then the gorilla-shaped henchman was passing a couple of cans through the window. Shortly, we were off again, with the Toyota trailing along behind. I wondered how much trouble they had getting service for the beast. I'd seen Datsun agencies in Mexico, but other Japanese cars did not seem to be well represented.

I sipped my beer, although I prefer coffee at that hour of the morning. I drove along easily, one-handed, while the barren-looking farms around the town gave way to the cactus desert once more. The traffic dwindled to nothing. There were just our two husky vehicles rolling along the endless road under the blue sky. I glanced at the mirror. Amado was keeping station a hundred yards back. Ramón took a sip of his beer. I hit the brakes hard, locking everything up tight, and throwing him against the windshield.

By the time the truck had slid to a halt, I had my revolver out. I drew the hammer back to full cock, and pushed the weapon into his side.

"Keep your hands in plain sight, you treacherous sonofabitch," I said. "Now we wait for that gofer of yours."

There were footsteps outside the carryall. Something cold touched the back of my head.

"Drop the gun, *Señor*," said Amado's voice through the open window. "Drop it or I will shoot."

twenty-two ....

I heard a car approaching from the north. It slowed a bit to pass the two vehicles crookedly stopped on the pavement; then it accelerated hard, receding into the distance ahead. The Mexican driver of the battered heap had either caught a glimpse of a firearm, or had simply disliked the looks of our little party. Whether it was a private holdup, a police arrest, or a military matter, he wasn't about to hang around and watch the show.

"It is a submachine gun," Ramón said. "It will remove your head from your shoulders if I give the word. So let me have your little revolver, *por favor*."

I grinned at him, unmoving, holding the Smith and Wesson hard against his side. "One of those Argentine greaseguns we saw the other morning, I suppose? The 9mm Luger Parabellum pistol cartridge, about thirty to the clip, right? That would really scramble a guy's brains, wouldn't it? Ramón, you're a fool. How long do you think you'll last after he pulls his trigger."

Ramón licked his lips. "You are bluffing. Are you willing to die in order to—"

I said harshly, "Hell, you've been trying to kill me for a couple of days. This way, at least I get to take you with me. Go ahead. Tell him to fire. Have you ever seen a man shot through the head, or anywhere else for that matter? He twitches, right? Do you know what the trigger pull of this weapon is, cocked? Barely two pounds. Just how many twitches do you think it will take, my dear friend and colleague? And you may have heard a lot of bull about the inadequacy of the .38 Special cartridge, but at contact range I guarantee that the bullet will blast a hole clear through your lungs from side to side, taking half your heart with it. If that's what you want, tell your gofer to shoot."

There was a tense little pause. Ramón seized upon the unfamiliar term. "Gofer. What is that word, gofer?"

"He's the man who goes for things," I said. "Things like beer across the street. Did the message get out, *amigo*? Did Amado manage to send word to Ernemann from Ciudad Constitucion, back there where you had us stop for gas, that Díaz will be landing his plane—well, O'Hearn's plane, complete with O'Hearn's pilot, and bodyguard—at Hotel Cabo San Lucas at eight tomorrow morning?" I grinned at him wolfishly. "Sure. I fed you the information hoping you'd pass it along to your imported hitman, and that's exactly what you did, isn't it?"

His face told me I was right. "You won't live to take advantage of—"

"I'll live," I said, I hope confidently. "You're playing in the wrong league now, *Señor* Solana-Ruiz. It's back to the minors for you. There was a time when I thought you were pretty hot stuff; but either I was mistaken or something's happened to you since we last met. I remember you using yourself for bait once, deliberately sticking your neck way out for your job and duty, but you wouldn't do that now, would you? Now you're trying to do things the safe and easy way. What happened? Did you get married and start a family? That's often the end of a good agent;

suddenly he feels he's just got to keep on living for the wife and kiddies, and he can't face the big risks any longer. Is that the way it was?"

"I am not married," Ramón said stiffly. "I do not know what you mean."

"Sure you do," I said. "No, keep your hands right on the dashboard. . . . Sure you know why you're trying to get other men to do the dangerous work for you these days. Work like killing me. Hell, if you'd done it yourself, you could have had me the first day and never risked a thing. I suspected nothing from my good friend Ramón, the man who'd once saved my life, the man who'd just called out the troops to help me across the border. . . . But that's why you helped me, isn't it, so you'd have me in your hands all unsuspecting? But then you found you couldn't bring yourself to do it face to face, not with me armed and all hopped up from dealing with Euler, ready to take on all comers. I should have guessed something was wrong all along. You finally set up a two-man ambush on the beach; and when that didn't work you tried to trick a bunch of tough revolutionaries into doing the job for you." I regarded him bleakly. "No, no, my friend. You're not going to sacrifice your precious life now just to kill me, not a chance. I'm as safe as if I were home in bed. So tell your boy to lay down that toy *ametralladora* or *fusil automatica* or whatever you call it down here. Tell him to place it very gently on the hood of the truck and step away from it. Remember, as long as we sit here like this, you're two pounds from dead—that's less than a kilo by your reckoning."

The actual trigger pull was four pounds. You don't generally hone it down to two on any weapon heavier than a .22 target pistol, but he didn't have to know that. I sat there and watched him—watched him die inside.

He licked his gray lips. "You are crazy, Matthew. The advantage is all mine—"

"No," I said. "It's all mine. Because I know that you

want me dead to protect the man you hired to get Díaz for you. Maybe you even promised Ernemann you'd take me off his back if the bank account trick didn't work; maybe that was part of the deal. But you know I have no real reason to want you dead. Okay, so you tried to have me murdered a little, but I don't spend time on petty revenge when there's work to be done." I started to shake my head, but Amado's gun muzzle discouraged the gesture, so I just said, "No, I can't afford to give in. If I do, you'll shoot me right here, now that you know I know where you stand. But you can yield without anybody getting hurt. Be smart, Ramón. It's the only way either of us will get out of this alive."

"If I give the order, how do I know you won't—"

I said irritably, "You're not thinking, damn it! If I wanted you dead, you'd be dead now, wouldn't you? I'd have shot you while you were still picking yourself off the windshield, and then I'd have gunned this heap to hell out of here. Amado would never have got close, not with his feeble little Toyota six against my big Chevy V8. If I wanted you dead, if I wanted to go around killing Mexican agents, do you think I'd have deliberately put myself into this kind of a hairy standoff?"

There was a lengthy silence. Motionless, the carryall was getting hot and stuffy in the desert sun. Another car drove by; the driver took a look, and blasted away in panic.

"Amado." Ramón cleared his throat. "Amado. . . ."

The henchman's voice was expressionless. "What is the command, *jefe?*"

"Lay it on the hood of the vehicle, Amado. Lay it down and step away from it. . . ."

It was no time for deep sighs of relief or the mopping of sweaty brows. There were still some tricky moments during which it helped me to be thought a nerveless human calculating machine, totally immune to fear. Under ordinary circumstances I'd have used a needle and a painless injection we have that keeps people asleep for about four hours—there are other injections with more permanent effects—but I'd left my drug kit way back in Santa Fe, New Mexico. Fortunately I still had the big roll of tape I'd bought for another purpose.

I got us off the road where we could work without being quite so much in the public view. I had Ramón tape up Amado, hands aft. I checked his work, and had him help his bound gorilla into the rear of the carryall. Then I taped up Ramón, hands forward, and put him into the passenger's seat. Finally, I went up to the Toyota and, after figuring out the manual gearshift, drove it off the highway and parked it out among the cacti where it would attract less attention.

I was about to lock it up and leave it when the thought came to me that if Ramón had been in touch with Ernemann—as he apparently had been—he might very well have described my vehicle; he was less likely to have described his own. I sighed, and drove the Toyota over to the Chevy and, with considerable labor, transferred all passengers and luggage.

Then I could afford, at last, to give that long-postponed sigh of relief and dry my face with my handkerchief as I drove us away. I could see, in the mirror, my large blue vehicle standing deserted by the roadside behind me. I wondered what my chances were of getting it back intact, assuming, of course, that I survived the next few hours, or days. Well, sacrifices are expected in the line of duty.

Ramón was silent beside me. It was too bad, in a way. Even though it had saved my life more than once on this safari, it was too bad. I once knew a singer, a terrific baritone with Metropolitan ambitions, whose voice left him suddenly for no apparent reason. And there was the sports car driver I remembered, headed for the big time, who cracked up badly and, although his injuries seemed to heal all right, never quite managed to win another race. Something had gone and he could never get it back.

"It was an ambush." Ramón's soft voice answered my thoughts. "The *insurgentes* were careless; they left me for dead, but I was not quite dead. But I could never afterwards. . . . I have often wished. . . ." He didn't finish. I didn't speak. After a while he asked, "How did you come to suspect me?"

"You couldn't find anything," I said. "A well-known professional murderer and a pretty girl agent were both wandering through his country, and the efficient *Señor* Solana-Ruiz knew nothing, nothing. Hell, when the colonel and the marquis got on the horn just now, they had all the information about Ernemann they needed inside four hours; but you'd investigated for days and come up with zilch, or so you would have me believe. So what were you hiding from your old Yankee friend besides a revolution or two? Well, perfect frankness is rare between agents of different nationalities, and I didn't really suspect you of anything but an acute attack of security-consciousness until I got to those interesting dunes by Laguna de la Muerte. Again, inefficiency; you were supposed to cover me and I almost got killed. That wasn't the Ramón I used to know, particularly when you seemed more concerned about the men I'd shot than about my welfare. Of course, you made a brilliant retrieve with those IDs, proving that the Bureau of Internal Security was responsible; and you got a strong assist from Mrs. O'Hearn who obligingly went hysterical and tried to blast me full of holes—something you weren't slow to take advantage of. You'd been trying to throw suspicion on the lady all along to keep me from wondering about you. But there was one thing that didn't quite fit the BIS story you were trying to sell me."

"What was that one thing, *amigo?*"

I said, "We've got a bunch of two-fisted shooters up in

the States these days. They've forgotten that the pistol was originally designed for one-hand use; they're so accustomed to clapping that second hand around the revolver butt that if you tied it behind them they'd die of frustration. I watched a BIS man in action just the other day. It never once occurred to him that if God had meant us to shoot a pistol two-handed, He'd have put two handles on it. Yet one of those ambush characters caught me with an empty gun, he had time to set himself for a good shot, and he just stuck out his hand—his one hand—and fired. It made me wonder a bit. It wasn't quite the way our great Bureau of Internal Security does its shooting."

Ramón hesitated. "But the identifications, they were quite genuine."

"Sure," I said, watching the black road sliding towards me in the sunshine that made it gleam like silver where it wound through the hills ahead. "But of course I never got to compare the pictures with the faces. And then Norma turned up and told a very interesting story about how she was almost kidnaped by two characters in Tijuana. I started thinking: what if those had been Euler's men—we speculated that he might have taken the risk of sending somebody across the border after her, remember? And suppose you weren't as totally ignorant about our girl's wanderings as you'd claimed. Suppose you'd actually had her under surveillance in Tijuana, and you'd nabbed the BIS boys when they made their play, but Norma got away in the shuffle. There would be two nice authentic IDs for you to use as you pleased. What did you do with the bearers?"

Ramón shrugged resignedly. "They are unharmed. They are being held in Ensenada, under arrest."

I guided the Toyota out to the edge of the two-lane pavement to give room to a large oncoming semi with *Carmelita* painted on the front bumper in ornate letters.

I said, "As for those mercenary military characters and stray aristocrats who'd somehow got the idea I'd been imported to shoot their pet general, it wasn't hard to sell them that notion by a handy informant, was it? Particularly after you left your muscleman hanging around conspicuously to 'protect' me, demonstrating how very important I was to you. A little tough on Amado, but as you say, he's got a hard head. Unfortunately, instead of shooting me as you'd hoped, or locking me up for the duration, they let me talk them around, and in the process I picked up some interesting information. I'd started asking myself a lot of questions. It had seemed a little strange that you'd be so eager to help us dispose of Ernemann, once I started to think about it. After all, the guy was doing exactly what you needed done. He was going to kill Díaz and thereby drop a big rock into the delicate revolutionary works. So why were you helping us stop him? Or were you?"

"I can see how you might wonder," Ramón said dryly. "I was afraid the question would occur to you before I could . . . dispose of you."

"There was just one problem," I said. "Where would a Mexican agent find dollars in the thousands, and tens and hundreds of thousands, for hiring an expensive gunman and framing anyone who threatened to interfere with his work?"

"I did not frame you," Ramón said. "That business you and your chief have mentioned, about the banks up in the United States, I know nothing about it."

"Well, okay, say Ernemann did it on his own with money you gave him, that's still a wad of cash. Governments don't dish out that kind of dough happily for far-out and controversial projects like assassination, so where did it come from? Colonel Huntington gave me a clue. There are, apparently, a good many wealthy Americans who are already settled comfortably in Baja California Sur and like it the way it is. They want no part of the Sanctuary Corporation and its military schemes. It occurred to me that in your desperate straits, trying to stop a revolution almost single-handed, you might have approached these people for funds and other help. And I remembered that in Mulege you'd chatted with a gent who looked like an American but spoke Spanish like a native; a gent who was apparently helping you in some kind of intelligence capacity." Again his face told me I had the right answer. I said, "Just one more thing. In all this mess have you come across a Chinese gent called Mr. Soo?"

He frowned quickly. "Soo? No I have heard no such. . . ." He stopped, and glanced at me, and shrugged. "I suppose it makes no difference now. Ernemann was seen to make rendezvous briefly with an unidentified Oriental in La Paz. That is all I know, and I cannot tell you what it signifies." He hesitated. "There is one question you have not asked, Matthew."

"What's that?"

"You have not asked why I had to hire a gunman to remove General Hernando Díaz. After all, I am considered fairly proficient with firearms myself."

I said carefully, "There could be political reasons. A Mexican general shot by a Mexican agent would be difficult to explain."

"But by the time explanations were required, Díaz would be dead and his revolution would be stopped and my task would be accomplished. No, my friend, I thank you for being diplomatic, but that is not the answer. The answer is that if I had tried to shoot the general, my hand would have shaken so badly that I would have missed."

That evening we were in Cabo San Lucas.

twenty-three •••••••••••••••••••

The little town of Cabo San Lucas is on the tip of the Baja peninsula, right at land's end. It boasts, on the rocky point behind it, an elaborate new hotel named Finisterra. There's a small harbor and a landing for the seagoing ferry that'll take you to Puerta Vallarta, some four hundred miles to the southeast on the Mexican mainland. I picked up a few supplies in the little store marked *Abbarotes* and hurried to return to the Toyota I'd parked some distance away, before my prisoners worked themselves free or a curious kid peeked inside and discovered them.

Finding everything under control, I got in and headed towards the Hotel Cabo San Lucas, which is located ten miles back up the highway from the town and the cape from which it takes its name. I didn't drive all the way back there, however. The 4WD Toyota, while not as big or conspicuous as my Chevy, was fairly distinctive in its own right, and I didn't want to keep it shuttling past the place repeatedly in case someone was watching the road. Anyway, driving by on the way down, I'd learned everything about it that could be learned from the road. I'd learned that the hotel itself was a handsome, rambling establishment clinging to the steep rocky shore below the highway. The airstrip was on the high ground on the other side of the road, almost invisible from a passing car. I might have had trouble spotting its exact location if a small plane hadn't come in for a landing just as we drove by.

Now I swung left across the pavement before I could see the hotel ahead—or be seen from it—and eased the Toyota down the highway embankment. I proceeded across country, heading inland, dodging cacti and thorny bushes, following a stony ridge that wouldn't show much in the way of tracks in case somebody came looking. When things got too rough, I swung down into the wide, sandy arroyo to the east. Starting up it, I felt the rear wheels dig in—I'd forgotten that with this vehicle you had to make a conscious effort to get four-wheel drive. I pushed and hauled at the pair of levers sprouting from the floor until I thought I'd set up the right combination, but she still wouldn't go. At last I remembered, and got out and locked the hubs of the front wheels. That fixed it, and we proceeded up through the brush until the arroyo narrowed and the spiny vegetation got so thick it would have taken a tank or bulldozer to make further progress. The Mexican-style odometer said I'd come about three kilometers, or a little over a mile and a half.

I put the blocky wagon under a small tree, switched off the ignition, and sat there for a little, listening. There were only the buzzings of occasional insects, and the distant sounds of cars on the highway behind us. So far, so good.

I got out and went back and dropped the tailgate and looked at my passengers lying neatly side by side—I'd put Ramón back there, gagged, before parking on the outskirts of the town. I went forward and picked up one of the Argentine squirt guns and the bag of groceries, returned, and set the bag on the tailgate. I dragged Ramón a little to the rear; then, holding the chopper one-handed —it was heavier than it looked—I reached into my pocket and got out my knife and flicked it open.

"Hold out your wrists," I said, and cut him free. "Now you can take your gag off, and Amado's, and you can free Amado's wrists, but the ankles stay taped. There's beer and bread and meat and cheese in the bag. There's also another of these pea-shooters up forward, and your personal artillery, in case you've got an uncontrollable yearning for firearms. I hope you go for one of the guns. I'm being stupid and sentimental, keeping you alive. Just give me one small excuse and I'll fix that. Okay?"

It had been a long, hot, uncomfortable ride, and it took them a while to work the kinks out, take care of the biological functions, and partake of nourishment. There was no conversation to amount to anything. I kept my eyes mostly on Amado, the well-trained human gorilla who'd never been left for dead anywhere, or if he had, it hadn't bothered him much. He was ready to jump me, hobbles or no hobbles, submachine gun or no submachine gun, if I gave him a chance, so I was careful not to. At last I had Ramón tie him up again, using clothesline I'd bought at the grocery since the tape supply had run out. Of course, you can't buy real clothesline any more, not even in deepest Baja. This was slick, white stuff—a plastic sheath around a rope core—but it seemed to have plenty of strength. I took care to check Ramón's knots, however, and I double-checked my own.

"I won't gag you," I said. "Out here you can yell all you want to. Be my guests."

I made myself a sandwich and opened a beer and sat down on a corner of the tailgate to have my supper, out of reach of a kick from my captives. The sun was getting well down in the sky, I noticed. I didn't have too much time if I was going to study the airstrip by daylight. On the other hand, it was going to be a long night; I didn't want to start my vigil sooner than absolutely necessary. I was aware that Ramón was watching me.

"Matthew."

"Yes."

"Your assignment is Ernemann, is it not?"

"Right," I said.

"You have no orders to protect Díaz."

"Right."

"You can shoot when it suits you. If . . . if you were to wait until after he has finished. . . ." Ramón stopped.

I was working on my second beer and my second sandwich; no sense steaming into action with insufficient fuel. I glanced at him irritably.

"Ernemann is a pro," I said. "You're suggesting that I play a game of tag with the rattlesnake before I chop its head off. Can you give me one good reason why I should make my assignment more difficult and dangerous just to oblige a gent who's done his damndest to have me murdered?"

There was a little silence; then it came, what I'd hoped I wouldn't have to hear: "There is one."

"Name it."

"You forget. We hold the *Señora* O'Hearn."

I finished my beer and gathered up my two bottles and Ramón's one. I went over and retrieved the one Amado had tossed into the brush in his usual sloppy fashion. I guess I was making amends for the two cans I'd used for target practice that morning and left behind, although it seemed a little screwy to be worrying about ecology while embarking on homicide. I stuffed all the bottles back into the grocery bag. Then I looked down at Ramón once more.

"I hope I'm not reading you right," I said. "Spell it out."

"If Díaz lives, Mrs. O'Hearn dies."

I sighed. "And another man just told me: if Díaz dies, Norma dies. You damned hostage peddlers are really putting the heat on me from all sides, aren't you?"

"I mean it! I left orders."

I regarded him for a moment longer; then I shoved his feet out of the way and slammed the tailgate shut. Five minutes later I was hiking off with the bolt-action .270 slung over my shoulder, a box of cartridges in my pocket, and my hands full of everything from groceries to submachine guns. Half a mile from the car, I unloaded the extraneous material I hadn't dared leave behind because the prisoners might have made use of it. A determined man can cut a lot of tape and rope with a broken beer bottle.

I thumbed five rounds into the magazine of the Remington, slipped one into the chamber, and pressed down the top cartridge in the magazine so the bolt would slide closed over it. I took my bearings from the setting sun and continued my cross-country journey. It was the prickliest damned country I'd ever hiked through. I felt like a human pincushion by the time I reached the airstrip, but I hit it just about where I'd planned, near the inland end. It was a shallow valley, the bottom of which had been flattened and smoothed to make the usual unpaved runway, aimed south towards the ocean.

I crouched in the brush, studying the situation. With the prevailing northerly winds, a landing plane would have to make its approach from seaward, coming in over the shore, past the hotel and the highway, touching down near the small buildings and tied-down planes at the south end of the strip, and rolling inland until it had lost speed enough to be able to swing around and taxi back. Well, there was nothing in that for me. To be sure, around the north end where I was, there was only brush and cactus. A machine-gunner hiding there could hose down a taxiing plane as it turned, and be gone into the boondocks—to a waiting jeep, say—before anybody could reach him from the inhabited end of the runway.

However, Ernemann was supposed to be an expert and conscientious workman. I was willing to gamble that he wouldn't do his job by simply spraying lead all over a bunch of unidentified people in an airplane. A perfectionist, he'd wait until they unloaded, and he could concentrate his fire on the specific target for which he was being paid.

It took me a while to work it out. I wished for a pair of binoculars, and I wished I knew a little more about automatic weapons and their requirements—I tend to be a one-shot specialist myself. It was almost dark before I'd decided on the two or three locations an experienced chopper man might pick within range of the debarkation area. Then I had to select a spot within easy rifle range; a sheltered spot from which I could pick off a man in any of those locations. . . .

He came well after midnight. I was sitting in my impromptu blind on the hillside below the rudimentary ridge overlooking the landing strip and the tethered planes. Suddenly I found myself wide awake, knowing that something had changed in the night. There was movement on the slope behind me and to the left. It occurred to me that if Ernemann knew I was there and had come stalking me, the advantage was all his. If he had the kind of chopper or automatic rifle he was reputed to favor, he was all set for night fighting, while my scope-sighted weapon was blind and almost useless in the dark. I reassured myself with the thought that he'd be unlikely to start a lot of shooting now since it would spoil his chances of accomplishing his mission in the morning.

I sat unmoving in my hidey-hole, listening hard. The faint sounds of his progress passed well inland of me. At last, after chasing a name for over a thousand miles, I saw him: a shadowy, crouching form slipping along the edge of the airstrip below and, finally, ducking back into the brush at just about the spot—well, one of the spots—I'd thought he might pick. The night was quiet again. It was time to take out the final problems and wrestle with them, facing the fact that a simple touch, as we call it, had turned into a complex matter with all kinds of personal and international ramifications.

Sentimentally considered, the decision I had to make was a terrible one. I had to decide which of two ladies whose favors I had enjoyed, to use the old-fashioned phrase, was to die. A TV hero would, I suppose, have built this up into a dreadful moral predicament. Actually, it was quite irrelevant. Our basic instructions are quite clear on the subject. As Norma herself had pointed out, we just don't play that game. Norma was in Baja under orders. Clarissa had involved herself from choice. They would both have to take their chances. I couldn't afford to consider them any more than I could afford to base my decision, much as I would have liked to, on the fact that the elegant Marquis had slapped my face. I wasn't a private individual here, goddamn it, with private decisions to make; I was an agent of national policy, if I could just figure out what the hell national policy was in this particular case.

The big question was, granted that I'd been sent here to take out Ernemann, since I might have a choice would Washington prefer to have me work it so Díaz wound up dead, or so he remained alive? It would seem that peace in the Americas, even though it involved the loss of a Mexican general, was a desirable goal. On the other hand, you can never tell about that crazy city on the Potomac, not to mention our fellow toilers in the underground vineyard with their fine estate in Virginia. Hell, for all I knew, the whole Sanctuary Corporation, for all its impressive membership and proclaimed elitist purposes, was just another spook shop like various captive airlines and trading companies around the world, and we'd been engaged specifically to keep Ernemann from interfering with its carefully planned little jewel of a revolution. . . .

I didn't seem to be coming up with any answers, and suddenly I knew why. My subconscious was trying to tell me that I was busily engaged in deep-frying my chicken legs while the bird was still running around the barnyard. Instinct was saying to hell with national policy, get your mind back to this Mexican thorn-bush-and-cactus slope on the double, Buster, because something is very, very wrong. And I knew what was wrong. It was the simple fact that nothing was wrong.

The whole thing was, I realized, much too good to be true. I'd driven the whole length of the Baja peninsula, planted myself behind a convenient bush, and my quarry had immediately and obligingly marched out and set himself down where I could shoot him the minute I had light enough to see. I mean, anybody who'd believe that would have a firm and unshakable belief in Santa Claus.

I realized that I was acting as if Ernemann were a dope instead of being, probably, the brightest private operator currently in the business. I was forgetting that he undoubtedly knew as much about me as I knew about him, and maybe a little more—after all, I didn't know just what weapon I'd be facing in his hands, but Ramón had certainly told him about the .270 that had been provided me complete with 4X scope. And still I was allowing myself to think that an experienced professional with this knowledge would deliberately put himself into a spot where an accurate long-range rifle anywhere on the hillside could pick him off like a clay pipe in a shooting gallery.

I drew a long breath and let it out. There was nothing for it but get the hell down there and see what had been so carefully stuck in front of me for a target. It took me the best part of an hour to cover the hundred and fifty yards in perfect—I hoped—silence. The last fifty yards, I had my little knife in my hand for any emergencies that might develop. Then I saw him sitting there, leaning forward a little against the weapon planted butt-down in front of him.

The silhouette of the gun was clear in the starlight. It was the Russian equivalent of the older German *Sturmgewehr*, or assault rifle, a kind of junior-grade BAR. Called the AK after its designer Kalashnikov, it's common in most communist and satellite countries. It's even made in Finland where it's called the M60. In China it's known as the Type 56. It's an ugly, businesslike, automatic weapon with a long, forward-curving magazine that takes a special, medium-powered 7.62 mm cartridge—.30 caliber to you—rating about halfway between the feeble pistol ammo used in short-range choppers such as Ramón's PAM-1s, and the big service round used in full-sized machineguns.

I had plenty of time to dwell on these technical considerations. The man didn't move. Supported by his weapon, he just sat there. I was toying with the uneasy notion that somebody had planted a hunched-over dummy for my benefit, when the shadowy figure gave a small start. I realized he'd been asleep. He was pretty good, however. He didn't throw any sudden, frantic looks around to see what might have sneaked up on him while he was snoozing. He just turned his head very warily, very slowly. . . .

He wasn't Ernemann.

twenty-four ....

There was no possible doubt about it. To be sure, I'd never met Ernemann; I knew him only from his dossier. However, one fact was pretty well established: the guy had impersonated me successfully at a couple of banks. Even though I wasn't a constant habitué of either institution, I do come from unmistakably European ancestry, and it seemed unlikely that even Andrew Euler with his violent prejudice could have accepted a frame-up based on a bank teller's description of an Asiatic gentleman calling himself Matthew Helm.

No, the Chinese before me was not Ernemann. Young and lean, he wasn't even a well-upholstered, moon-faced, middle-aged character sometimes called Mr. Soo. Well, he wouldn't be. Mr. Soo was not expendable, and this youth had obviously been placed here deliberately to draw my fire—Mr. Soo had never been hesitant about risking a little low-grade manpower in a good cause. Apparently, he'd supplied Ernemann with some live bait designed to draw my attention one way so the real expert could dispose of me safely from a totally different direc-

tion. But just what the hell was the link between Ernemann and Soo. . . .

I dismissed the question from my mind. There had
been too damned much heavy theoretical thinking already. It had almost got me killed. Right now I had an
important practical question to answer: whether or not I
should leave the bait alive, or use the knife in my hand. I
was tempted to use it. The idea that perhaps, eventually, I
would have to deal with two gents armed with fully automatic AK-type weapons—assuming Ernemann had
brought a spare—wasn't appealing, since I only had a
slow-firing bolt-action rifle.

On the other hand, this man was now my bait as well
as Ernemann's. As long as he behaved as expected, my
real quarry would remain unalarmed, I hoped, basking in
the security of his own cleverness. Thinking I'd fallen for
his trick, he'd be off guard. Well, maybe.

It took me most of another hour to withdraw silently
and reassess the situation, which was now, of course,
drastically changed. The great problems that had troubled
me were no longer relevant; I no longer had a choice. My
primary job was Ernemann, not a stray Chinese gunner—
what the hidden young gent did with his AK-47, or Type
56, or whatever variation he had, was no concern of
mine. If he was good enough to get Díaz when Díaz land-
ed, Díaz was dead. That meant, of course, that Norma
was also dead. *This is my assignment as well as
yours,* she'd said, *don't get any funny notions about me.*
Okay.

It was time for me to do what I should have done from
the start: get into Ernemann's mind and look at the situation from his point of view. Well, like me he had a specific objective, in his case, Díaz. I was simply an obstruction
he had to surmount on his way to this objective. That
meant that, as a man who took pride in his work, he
wouldn't trust a Chinese kid to accomplish alone the job

he, Ernemann, had been hired for. He'd place himself where he could deal with me if I showed, sure; but that spot would not be so far away from the plane-loading area that he couldn't back up his young assistant in case of need.

It became, then, a simple problem in ballistics. If he had another AK-47 or the equivalent—I'd have to gamble on that—the medium-powered cartridge in a hand-held automatic weapon would give him only a limited sure-kill range, say two hundred yards. Even that would have been stretching it far beyond the realm of certainty for me—I'm not all that good with the chatter-guns—but I was, after all, dealing with a specialist.

There was really not much choice. He had to station himself somewhere on the low ridge above the landing area; maybe directly above it, maybe thirty or forty yards either way, depending on how the field of fire looked from up there. From that position he could cover the whole slope and mow me down when I appeared somewhere below him, and he could also reach out, if needed, over the head of his Chinese gunner, and clean up after him if he goofed—or if I managed to get a bullet into the youth before he could get his weapon into action.

My ballistic problem was equally simple. With my high-powered rifle and telescopic sight, I had three or four hundred yards to play with—assuming I could find a solid rest to shoot from. As Colonel Huntington had mentioned, I'd once done a job at five hundred meters, but that had been a heavy-barreled target-type rifle with a powerful scope, and I'd worked with it for weeks, preparing for the assignment. With a light hunting rifle through which I'd got to fire no more than a dozen practice rounds, four hundred yards was absolute maximum, and I'd be happier with three hundred. Again, there was not much choice. The ridge rose to a little rocky knob inland. From there I could cover the length of it, no matter where my man placed himself along it. If I was lucky, I'd have a two-hundred-and-fifty-yard shot. If I was unlucky, it could be sixty or eighty yards longer.

It wasn't a bad spot, I decided, when I reached it. The brush gave me cover up there, and a flat rock made an ideal rest for my elbows. Using my knife, silently, I cut away a few branches that might have interfered. Then I settled down to wait. Even with the time I'd spent prowling around, it was a long night. This time, I didn't let myself think about anything as I sat—I remembered an Indian guide I'd once had who'd insisted that no white man was ever worth a damn as a hunter because he was always thinking about bills or business or women when he should have been thinking about deer or elk.

There was no movement down by the airfield. Maybe my young Chinese friend had gone to sleep again. I wondered if he knew he was a decoy, and decided he probably didn't; they work better if you keep them ignorant. There was a steady, muffled rumble of heavy machinery from one of the buildings at the end of the field. I'd already determined that it housed the generators that provided the hotel's electricity. Occasional cars drove by on the highway, invisible below the end of the runway, showing only the loom of their headlights. Very gradually, the sky became less intensely black in the east, and the stars began to fade. Some time later, the sun appeared.

At full daylight, a plane came in for a landing. I saw a little flash of sunlight off a gun barrel as the hidden youth changed his grip on his AK. Obviously, he'd never spent much time in a duck blind or he'd have learned to be more careful of that.

There was no sign of movement along the ridge. The plane, a single-motor job, swept in from the sea, used about two thirds of the runway, swung around, and taxied to within point-blank range of the Russian-type *Sturmgewehr* in the bushes. A single man got out, and the pilot handed down a couple of suitcases and a long fishing rod case. A battered old Plymouth station wagon appeared from the direction of the hotel. The driver got out and threw the luggage into the rear and drove off with the new arrival. The plane taxied away towards the ocean end of the runway, turned inland, and took off, disappearing over the desert to the north. At least, I reflected, the boy machine-gunner had self-control; he hadn't mowed down the first target that appeared, although it must have been a temptation.

More time passed. There was no sign of human life along the ridge; even the birds and rodents were playing elsewhere. Then there was another buzzing in the sky to the northeast. My watch read 8:03. This time I didn't look at the plane. I didn't look at the Chinese kid with his lethal toy. I just watched the ridge unblinkingly—well, as unblinkingly as my eyelids would allow. I heard the aircraft make its seaward turn, and caught a brief glimpse of it out there—a larger flying machine with two motors. Watching the ridge, I heard it touch down, make its run-out, turn, and come back.

For a moment, it sounded so close I had the feeling it was climbing the brushy slope towards me. Then the motors quit and I heard the door open. I braced myself for gunfire, but nothing happened. I watched the ridge, but the sound of conversation reached me with startling clarity considering the distance. Somebody was out of the plane, somebody who spoke English badly, with a strong Spanish accent. Díaz? Another voice joined the first, strictly American. O'Hearn?

O'Hearn's voice, if it was his, called loudly: "Come on, come on, you clumsy bastards, get those rods out here, the General wants to go fishing, dammit! Krakowski, stop fiddling with your lousy plane and lend a hand. . . ."

I risked a glance. There were two men on the ground. They were both heavy men, both in light trousers and gaudy sports shirts, but there the resemblance ended. It was easy to distinguish the red-faced American millionaire from the dark-faced, moustached Mexican general. A third man, also Mexican, got out of the plane and started receiving luggage passed him by a fourth, American, who wore a pilot's cap. Phil Krakowski, lover-boy for hire. Still there was no gunfire.

I returned my attention to the ridge. I heard a new American voice, presumably the pilot's, say something I couldn't make out, probably, that that was it, Mr. O'Hearn.

Clarissa's loudmouthed husband could be heard all over Baja. "Well, haul your ass over to the hotel, Phil, boy, and get us some transportation. They seem to be all asleep down there."

Krakowski acknowledged the command. I heard the sound of the plane door as he closed it behind him. There was a moment of silence; then the AK opened up.

The plane motor had sounded loud in the morning stillness; this noise was louder. It went on and on. No neat little three-shot bursts for our eager Chinese prodigy; he knew what a trigger was for, and he just clamped down on it and stayed clamped until the clip was empty. It seemed like a hell of a lot of shooting for the simple job of killing one man. I watched the ridge. Nothing stirred. I risked another glance to the side; and you've never seen anything like it since a certain St. Valentine's day.

They were all down, all four of them, and blood was running everywhere. Then, as I watched, one of the bodies moved. Oscar O'Hearn pulled himself painfully to his feet and staggered towards the buildings where people were now appearing. Fascinated, in a gruesome way, by his painful, bloody, weaving progress, I almost missed what I'd come a thousand miles to see. Suddenly there was my target, three hundred yards down the ridge. Ernemann had popped out of a patch of brush you wouldn't think could conceal a rabbit. He was kneeling with another Russian—or maybe Chinese—assault rifle at his shoulder, tracking the fleeing man. The gun began to speak.

I swung my Remington into line, waited until the cross-hairs settled in the right place, and let the piece fire when the trigger pressure reached the letoff point. After all that had gone before, the shot was easy enough. The chattering of the automatic weapon ceased and Ernemann sank back into the brush. A glance showed me that O'Hearn was sprawled by the runway, obviously dead.

"Very good," said a voice behind me. "Now the Oriental, *amigo,* please."

I glanced over my shoulder. Ramón was standing there with his little PAM-1 aimed at my midsection. Off to one side was Amado with the sister gun. They must have freed themselves somehow and tracked me to the spot where I'd dumped their artillery. I was aware of a new sound in the air. Another plane was landing. I saw that the Chinese youth was out in the open and running hard to intercept it at the inland end of the landing strip.

"Por favor," said Ramón very politely. "We cannot reach him but you can. Please shoot him before he reaches that airplane."

I did. The escape plane, finding no live customers, turned on full power and blasted out of there fast. Ramón was saying something congratulatory, but I turned away and walked down to take a look at the dead man who was supposed to look a little like me, enough to fool a bank teller, at least. I couldn't see the slightest resemblance.

twenty-five ....

Everybody was very sorry. There had been rumors of a proposed terrorist attempt against the life of a certain influential American industrialist visiting Baja, but detailed information had been received too late. Mexican and U.S. agents, working together, had arrived on the scene only in time to intercept and dispose of the ruthless international gangsters after they had done their bloody work. Tragically, that great Mexican patriot and military genius, General Hernando Díaz, who'd just happened to be on the same plane, had fallen victim to stray bullets from the assassins' guns. The nation mourned the loss of one of its most illustrious citizens. . . .

"Very neat," I said. "So the touch was aimed at O'Hearn; and Díaz's death was simply a regrettable accident, of no political significance whatever."

"Precisely," Ramón said. "It is all very satisfactory, *amigo.*"

We were having coffee in my luxurious room at the Hotel Cabo San Lucas, with a wall of glass looking out upon a tiny private patio surrounded by a high, vine-covered wall. The fact that there was a husky gent named Amado lounging in the patio was just part of the service, of course. After all, nobody knew what had happened to Mr. Soo or what his intentions were now. There was also the possibility of reprisals from the Sanctuary Corporation. I was not to think I was a prisoner under guard, heavens no; this was merely a precaution to preserve my valuable life.

"Well, I'm glad somebody's happy," I said. "You hired it done and it got done. Did it work all the way?"

"I think so," Ramón said. "The ships we were watching have turned away, presumably to discharge their lethal cargoes elsewhere. The training encampment in the desert is empty; the guerrillas have dispersed."

"Just because one man is dead. It seems like a very simple solution."

Ramón said, "As I told you before, my friend, a home-grown revolt by a recognized native leader at the head of dissident native troops—he did have a few that would have followed him—is one thing, commonplace these days, of no great international importance. Naked aggression by a military force, equipped and controlled by an association of wealthy foreigners, is something totally different." Ramón grimaced. "Of course we were all wealthy foreigners on this continent once, aggressing against the simple natives of the time. It was the standard method of changing the map of the world. It may become so again. But at the moment more polite international rules are in effect; and the Sanctuary Corporation has, I believe, conceded this round—which is not to say there won't be another, somewhere."

I hesitated. "What about the Frenchman?"

Ramón said without expression, "The Marquis de Beaupré, after a pleasant cruise in the Sea of Cortez, is returning with his chartered yacht to Acapulco." He paused. "To answer the question you did not ask: no female bodies have been found. But the Sea of Cortez is very deep."

"Sure." I looked at him bleakly. "With respect to the ladies, *you* were bluffing, weren't you?"

He smiled faintly. "Let us just say that it had not occurred to me to leave such detailed and gory instructions concerning the *Señora* O'Hearn." He shrugged apologetically. "I had to try, Matthew."

"Sure." After a moment, I asked, "Were you planning to double-cross Ernemann all the time, in your Machiavellian way?"

"You mean, have him shot after he had done his work for me?" Ramón shook his head. "No. If things had turned out as expected, I would have kept my bargain with him. He would have been paid in full and permitted to leave safely. If only the general had been shot, no one else, there would have been no way of concealing the fact that he was the real target, would there? And I assure you, Matthew, that I did *not* give orders to have three additional men killed just to make a plausible story for the press. I merely saw the possibilities after it had happened." He frowned. "I still do not understand the reason for the wholesale massacre."

I said, "Hell, turn a kid loose with a machine gun and anything can happen. Chinese, U.S., or Mexican, they just like to hear the damn things go rat-tat-tat."

"Yes, but—" Ramón shrugged. "Ah, well, it is over, at least for the time being. Your car is outside. Please do not think me inhospitable, but I feel it is better that you leave as soon as possible. Drive north and stop at the Hotel Mulege tonight; that is on the hill across the river from the Serenidad where we stayed before. You will be joined there by *Señora* O'Hearn. After a good night's rest, you will continue to drive north, with her. You can spend a second night in Ensenada, in the Bahia Hotel, since you are familiar with that establishment. Two gentlemen will

oin you there. You will return to them their wallets and
weapons which I will give you. You will warn them to
keep their security operations north of the border hence-
forth; next time we will not be so lenient. In the morning,
you will take the little road northeast to Tecate, and then
proceed east on Highway 2 past Mexicali to the little
town of San Luis. Cross the border there and discharge
your male passengers; the lady too, if she so wishes. Drive
slowly towards Yuma, some twenty miles north. I have
been told somebody will make contact with you along the
road."

"Arrest me, you mean," I said dryly. "I'm still officially a traitor, remember?"

"It is out of my jurisdiction, but my impression after
several long-distance telephone conversations is that
there have been some changes in that situation. I have
been told to advise you not to act hastily, once across the
border." He hesitated. "Matthew."

"Yes?"

"Remember that it can happen to anyone."

I looked at him and saw that we were now talking
about something else. "Sure," I said. "I know."

He said, a little defensively, "I have been offered an
important administrative post—a reward for a discreet
and successful operation. I will take it, of course." He set
his coffee cup aside and rose and held out his hand.
"*Adíos, amigo.*"

"*Adios.*"

Taking his hand, rising, I knew that this time it was a
real good-bye. We wouldn't meet again, at least not in
the line of business. He was leaving the real life-and-
death world of the undercover agent for the unreal, safe,
artificial existence people call civilized, that survives only
through the efforts of uncivilized characters like us. . . .

Two days later I approached the border crossing at San
Luis feeling more like a tour-bus driver than a secret
agent. With four on board, the truck seemed crowded in

spite of its size, not that it really mattered. Clarissa and I had had a day and a couple of nights alone to sort things out, but we hadn't managed too well. After all, she was now the wealthy Widow O'Hearn, and I was a guy who'd cold-bloodedly sacrificed a helpless female assistant to get a job done. Things had changed for both of us, somehow. While I won't say we were actively mourning our dead, they did seem to have an inhibiting effect on our relationship.

So the lack of privacy wasn't significant, but the two BIS men we'd picked up in Ensenada were self-righteous creeps who acted deeply injured because some crummy Spanish-speaking officials had had the nerve to get legalistic about a lousy little international border, for Christ's sake! It was the natural reaction of humorless men who'd been caught trying to snitch fruit out of the neighbor's melon patch; but it made them even worse company than they would have been otherwise. It was a pleasure to get them out of the car after passing customs, even though they made a beeline for the nearest phone.

I said, "In spite of what Ramón said about a changed situation, I'm betting they're calling somebody to come and arrest me, figuring it'll give them a few points on the credit side of the ledger to balance against the disgrace of being caught in Mexico." I glanced at the girl beside me. "You're allowed to get out here if you want."

She gave me a wry little smile. "I was in at the start, Matt. I'll stay for the finish, if you don't mind."

"Suit yourself."

We drove north towards Yuma. Presently a big white station wagon came alongside. When I looked that way, the driver, whom I recognized as Gregory Kotis, signaled me to follow him. He pulled ahead and, presently, turned off the main road onto a small dirt track heading off across the Arizona landscape. We drove for about fifteen miles, until we came to what seemed to be an ordinary, rather shabby, cluster of ranch buildings. Kotis parked his

ar beside the barn, which was a little larger than you'd
xpect—they don't generally use Pennsylvania-sized barns
n that arid country. I stopped the truck alongside. Kotis
.ot out and came to my window.

"Good afternoon, Mrs. O'Hearn," he said politely. "I
vas very sorry to hear about your husband. . . . This is
.ot an arrest, Helm, so please don't do anything sudden
.nd violent. We've already lost several men to your ex-
.losive organization; we'd rather not lose any more."
When I didn't say anything, he went on: "I just thought
.ou'd like to see our secret installation, the one you were
.o curious about. The one where your colleague, er, died.
. . You may come, too, if you like, Mrs. O'Hearn."

The big barn door had a smaller door in it, which
.pened as we approached. An armed guard with a hol-
tered .45 automatic stepped back to let us pass. Inside,
.here was a long hall with several open doors on each
.ide. The rooms into which I looked were all empty.

"Detention cells to the left," said Kotis. "Interrogation
.oom, sick bay, and offices to the right. You saw the liv-
.ng quarters for the personnel: the ranch house outside."

Clarissa asked, puzzled: "But what is it, really?"

Kotis looked embarrassed. He spoke without looking at
.ither of us: "If you're told often enough, strongly
.nough, that the safety of the nation is at stake, you tend
.o accept methods that are not quite. . . . No, I won't ex-
.use myself. I knew it was wrong. The dirty fact is that I
.imply followed orders because it was easier than ques-
.ioning them. Like Eichmann, I suppose. The new direc-
.or of the Bureau has given instructions to dismantle this
.lace and the two others like it located in other areas."

"The new director?" I said.

"Yes. The appointment has not been officially con-
.rmed yet, so I'd better not mention the name. . . . You
.ere right, of course, Helm."

"Right about what?"

"The bullet that killed the guard did not come from the

guard's gun, a .45. The reports had been misplaced deliberately, and I had a difficult time tracking them down, but I finally discovered them in an obscure file . . . well, never mind that. The important fact they disclosed was that the guard had been shot by a service .38 Special, the kind of weapon issued to all our agents—and to Andrew Euler. In here, please."

The room we entered was obviously designed for medical purposes. It had glass-front metal cabinets along the walls, a stainless steel examining table, a sterilizer, oxygen apparatus, and the usual fancy lights and appliances. There were three men in the room. Two had white coats on. One was thin, with big horn-rimmed glasses; the other was a bullet-headed bruiser. The third man, in hospital pajamas, was Andrew Euler. He was sitting in a chair looking gray and shrunken and disheveled. His eyes seemed even more unfocused and uncertain than I remembered.

"We have to watch him," Kotis said softly. "He keeps trying to kill himself. He says the guilt is too great to bear."

The thin man with the glasses said, "At the moment, he is heavily tranquilized."

"I feel somewhat responsible," Kotis said. "I couldn't forget what you'd told me, Helm. I made some discreet investigations. When I finally managed to learn about the weapons, the next thing I knew, Mr. Euler had taken an overdose of sleeping pills, leaving a vague and rambling confession that we still don't quite understand." He hesitated. "Your warning was unnecessary. Nobody tried to harm me."

I looked at the man in the chair. "I guess he felt there had been enough killing," I said. "But I couldn't be sure of that; I had to warn you."

Clarissa stirred. "I don't understand about the guns."

Kotis said, "Tell her, Helm."

"Roger . . . Jack, your brother, was supposed to have

grabbed a gun from his guard's holster and, before he was killed, shot down four people including the guard himself, hospitalized with a bullet in the head."

"He died two days ago," Kotis said.

I said, "It didn't make sense to me. If you grab a gun from a guard's belt holster and pull the trigger, the bullet may go into the guts, it may go as high as the chest, but it isn't likely to wind up in the head. Not unless there's a wrestling match with the weapon waving around, and nothing of the sort was mentioned. Anyway, there wasn't time for much of a struggle, with other men right in the room. My feeling was, Roger wasn't interested in the guard except for the weapon he carried; he'd just grab the gun, boot the guy across the room, and get on with the work that really intrigued him. But if he had taken out the guard first, the man would have been shot with his own gun, right?"

"Well, yes," said Clarissa. "But then who . . . why . . ."

I said, "It's really very simple. Think of the two main characters involved. Mr. Euler first. He's kind of a naive gent who gets his ideas of human behavior, it seems, chiefly from TV. He'd been having Roger questioned and getting nothing because there was nothing to get. All Euler really had on him was a little money in the bank that could have been put there by anybody, and a shaky deposition from an informer with a lousy reputation for veracity—"

"Groening has renounced his sworn statement," Kotis said.

"Sure," I said. "Yet remember, Roger represented something Mr. Euler considered a blot on the moral escutcheon of this great nation, something evil to be wiped out any way possible. And Mr. Euler isn't beyond using a little evil to wipe out evil, like a lot of fanatics. Look at these fairly undemocratic interrogation centers he's set up to save democracy. Where Roger was concerned, evidence of guilt was needed, and Euler figured flight would be sufficient evidence of guilt. It looked very simple from Euler's naive point of view—remember, this is a man who doesn't know what the killing business is all about. All he knows is that he thinks it's terrible. He figured he'd just arrange to let Roger grab a gun; and then Roger, like a sensible man, would hold up the others in the room, maybe tie them up, and make his escape—but of course Euler would have people kind of casually stationed at all the exits. He figured, in his innocent TV way, that nobody'd be hurt. Faced with overwhelming force, Roger would simply surrender his stolen gun without firing a shot, but the escape attempt would be on the record, black and incriminating."

"Mad!" It was Euler's voice. "He was a madman! How could I guess he would simply murder—"

"The trouble was," I said, "Roger didn't watch TV. He didn't know how he was supposed to behave. He just knew that he was angry as hell and getting angrier. He wanted a gun for just one reason—to burn down the sadistic bastards who'd been humiliating and tormenting him. . . . Just who were the three who got shot, besides the guard, Kotis?"

"Two interrogators and a doctor."

"In other words, two beat-'em-up specialists and the guy with the needle full of scopolamine, right?"

Kotis hesitated. "Well, scopolamine isn't really used much any longer—"

I said, "Look at it from Roger's point of view. We have to take that kind of crap from our enemies, sometimes. We've all been through that wringer. To have it done to us by self-righteous, self-styled patriots who are supposed to be on our side is a little more than we can be expected to take with equanimity. . . . Roger put up with it for a while, but he was getting closer and closer to the detonation point as it went on. Finally, somebody left a gun handy, and that was that. He didn't expect to escape. He knew damned well why the weapon had been made available to him—that careless-guard gambit has whiskers on it. He knew they were waiting for him out in the hall. But the guys he wanted weren't out in the hall; and by this time he was so furious he was ready to go out if he could just take them with him. Which is exactly what he did."

Euler made an ugly little whimpering noise. "How could I know. . . ."

I said, "So there was Euler, waiting for his escaping prisoner out in the hall, when all hell broke loose in the interrogation chamber. That hadn't been in the TV script at all. Euler charged in there with you, Kotis, and found Roger busily performing his neat triple execution. Blood and dead men everywhere, a terrible disaster instead of a cleverly frustrated escape, and huddled in the corner was the guard staring at him, Euler, with big accusing eyes, obviously ready to announce the name of the person who'd ordered him to be so careless with his weapon. More men were charging in, guns were firing, and in the middle of the confusion, the non-violent Mr. Euler yielded to a primitive sense of self-preservation and snapped a shot at the head of the man who could ruin him, maybe without even thinking about it consciously. . . ."

twenty-six ....

Yuma, Arizona, is a scorching hell-hole in summer, but in winter it's just a pleasantly sunny desert town surrounded by irrigated farm lands. The motel at which we stopped wasn't a Holiday Inn, but it might just as well have been. In a way, it was kind of pleasant to be back in good old plastic U.S.A., and we had a couple of martinis apiece to celebrate. Clarissa had changed out of her much-abused corduroys, perhaps for the last time; the long journey was at an end, and the once fashionable pantsuit had long since passed the point of no return. She wore her long Mexican dress and was the most striking woman in the chrome-plated dining room. The steaks weren't bad.

"Well, it's been a . . . a very educational experience," she said at last, and there was a little color in her cheeks as she said it. Then she said, "I suppose I should be sorry for that poor man, Euler, but I find it difficult. I guess I'm not a very forgiving person." When I didn't say anything, she glanced towards the door and went on: "I called

O'Hearn, Inc., from my room. They're sending a limousine to take me home to Scottsdale. I think it's probably waiting by now; I just saw somebody who looked like a chauffeur carrying my suitcase through the lobby. So . . . I guess it's good-bye, Matt. Thank you for one more dinner."

"I'll see you to the car," I said, and rose to help her with her chair. As we walked out of there, I said, "Leave it now, Clarissa."

She glanced at me sharply. "What do you mean?"

"Euler will be taken care of. For the rest of his life, until he manages to end it somehow. And you don't need to take care of me."

We were crossing the lobby. A uniformed man came forward, cap in hand. "Mrs. O'Hearn? The car is outside."

"Wait for me, please," she said. "I'll be along in a minute."

"Yes, ma'am."

She watched him go, and turned back to me. "Matt, I don't understand what you're trying to say."

"Cut it out, sweetheart," I said. "The Chinese boy with the assault rifle had a beautiful standing shot at Díaz, but he waited endlessly until the handsome pilot, Krakowski —the guy who'd toyed with your affections at your husband's request—got out of the plane to where he could be hit with certainty, too. Obviously, the kid's instructions involved more than Díaz. And then your husband got up, wounded, and started towards safety, and since the kid had shot his gun empty, Ernemann himself rose up and took the fatal risk—as it turned out—of finishing him off. Why bother with Oscar O'Hearn if the contract involved only Hernando Díaz? As you say, Mrs. O, you're not a forgiving person."

She stared at me, wide-eyed. "You can't be serious!"

There were people passing through the lobby, but they

gave us little attention, except the occasional male who couldn't help an admiring glance at the handsome lady in the Mexican dress.

I said, "There was always a question as to where all the money was coming from. Of course, you were quite truthful in telling me you had no designs on Díaz's life. As long as Díaz seemed to be the target, the only target, you had no adequate motive. But the way it turned out in the end, it became rather obvious that somebody had got to Ernemann, somebody besides Ramón Solana-Ruiz with the pennies he'd collected from his *Americano* friends in Baja, somebody with real money to throw around, somebody with influence enough in financial circles to pry the numbers of certain private bank accounts out of reluctant bank officials."

"Matt, stop it please. If this is supposed to be a . . . a parting joke, I think it's in very poor taste."

I said, "The person in question had obviously shown Ernemann how he could make a lot more profit for very little more trouble—all it would cost him would be a few additional rounds of ammunition. If he'd just traverse the automatic weapon a little farther while disposing of General Díaz, there would be a nice sum in a numbered Swiss bank account, say, in addition to what he was already collecting from Solana-Ruiz. Not to mention the extra cash needed to get certain U.S. operatives into trouble and off his trail, making the whole job that much easier."

She licked her lips. "This is insane! How would I even learn about a man like Ernemann and what he was up to?"

"Stop it, sweetheart, it's no good," I said mildly. "Your brother told you, of course. Hell, you were involved. Naturally, Roger—Jack—would warn his big sister that her husband was mixed up in dangerous foreign schemes involving dangerous revolutionaries threatened by dangerous foreign assassins. A deliberate breach of security, of course; but I gather the brother-sister relationship was fairly strong."

"But you're arguing against yourself! If our relationship was that strong, I'd never have dreamed of framing him into prison, my own brother—"

"Of course you would," I said. "It was the only sensible thing to do. If you were really going to hire Ernemann to take care of husband Oscar and lover-boy Phil, you'd want brother Jack put away where he couldn't spoil the plan—besides, you could tell yourself you were really doing it for his own good. You didn't want him killed, going up against a lethal guy like Ernemann. You figured he'd be safe in jail, and with all that money and all those company lawyers, you'd get him out afterwards free and clear, no sweat. Only, you didn't understand your brother as well as you thought, and you didn't know Andrew Euler at all, so that scheme backfired badly. But the rest went like clockwork, and Ernemann even had the grace to get himself shot by me after doing his job, saving you some money, no doubt, and the nagging worry about whether or not he would blackmail you for the rest of your life. You needn't have worried about that. Ernemann hadn't got where he was by putting the screws on his clients; he played it straight. But you won't find many men around of Ernemann's caliber. Now you'll have to use what you can pick up in some place like Las Vegas— now that you don't have experienced brother Jack to steer you around the underworld—and those boys will take you for every nickel you've got, assuming they can do the job, which they can't."

She licked her lips once more, watching me closely. "What job is that, Matt?"

I said, "Mrs. O, you're a very smart girl, but you're a goddamned amateur. Am I supposed not to know that you've been watching me like a stalking cat all through dinner—hell, all the way up from Mulege—wondering if I was safe to leave around, and if not what you should do about me since unfortunately you hadn't been able to manage the job during that nice phony display of submachine gun hysterics down by Laguna de la Muerte? Well, the answer is: nothing. Sit tight, doll. You're in the clear. This outfit of ours was organized to solve difficult, dirty, and dangerous problems on the national level. With all due respect, ma'am, a lady having her husband and lover —false lover—murdered is not all that important, at least not to us. Mow them down in rows, Mrs. O. We don't care. Just refrain from trying to frame any more of us into jail, please. You're perfectly safe, and you'll remain so unless you do something stupid like trying to hire me killed to shut my mouth. So leave it now. Just forget it. You've got it made. Don't spoil it by trying to make it perfect; it's damned good the way it is. Okay?"

She hesitated. There was a bright, cold, speculative look in her eyes as she studied my face. I remembered that her brother hadn't been the most well-balanced character I'd ever worked with. A wild streak ran in that family. Not that I'm criticizing; I've got a few streaks of my own.

She said without expression: "Aren't you forgetting something?"

"Like what?"

"All those hundred-dollar bills you were going to ram down somebody's throat or . . . or elsewhere." Before I could think of something to say, she stepped forward and kissed me hard on the mouth. "Good-bye, Matt. I don't think you're quite as tough as you talk."

She turned and strode away, straight and tall in the long, bright dress, a new woman and, I reflected, a fairly dangerous one. Well, the law enforcement problems of the nation, or the state of Arizona, were not my concern; and the shooting had occurred in Mexico, anyway. You couldn't say O'Hearn and Krakowski hadn't had it com-

ing. The trouble with people like that, as with people like
Euler, or the young, drunk, American campers in the van
that went off the road south of Mulege, is that they never
figure anybody's going to get mad enough to strike back.
They're always terribly surprised and hurt when the retaliators move into action.

When I got to my room, Mac was waiting in one of the
chairs by the window that would have looked out on the
pool if the heavy draperies hadn't been pulled across
them. He hadn't changed; he never did. He was still the
lean, gray-clad, gray-haired gent with the black eyebrows
for whom I'd worked longer than I cared to remember.
He looked like an investment broker unless you looked
closely and knew what you were looking for. Even then
you might not realize you were facing one of the half-
dozen most dangerous men in the world.

"There was a telephone call for you," he said. "The
desk said the gentleman would call back."

"Oh," I said, "It was a man?"

He regarded me for a moment. "If you're thinking of
Norma, the way you did it is the way it must be done," he
said quietly. "You know that, Eric. We cannot operate if
we are going to be vulnerable to the whims of anyone
who cares to point a gun at one of us. Eventually they
will learn it will get them nothing but trouble, and stop."

"Eventually is a long time," I said. I went over to the
dresser and opened the top drawer and returned to slap a
thick stack of bills onto the cocktail table beside him.
"Ten grand from Roger. Ten grand from me. I have another thirty in two separate accounts, I gather. It should
make a great Christmas party for the gang, if we went in
for Christmas parties."

Mac looked at me sharply. "Do you know the origin of
this money, Eric?"

"Yes."

"Should it be returned?"

"I don't think the lady expects it. In fact, I'm sure she's covered its disappearance very well, and would prefer not having to explain its return. She has plenty where it came from."

"I see." He thought for a moment. "Then I suggest you bank it all, declare it properly to the IRS, and once the taxes have been paid, bring me what remains and I will put it into our special contingency fund. Congress has not been too generous lately."

"Yes, sir." I put the wad of money back where I'd got it. "Now tell me about Soo."

"Mr. Soo has a large project in mind," he said, "somewhere on this continent, we are not yet quite sure what or where. Mr. Soo is a methodical man. He likes to remove any obstacles blocking his operations before they actually have a chance to obstruct him. Being Oriental, he is handicapped; his own trained people cannot move inconspicuously in the western world. He therefore decided to hire a European specialist for this particular assignment."

"What assignment?" I asked. "Who's the obstacle—" I stopped, beginning to realize belatedly just what U.S. interest Mac had been protecting when he sent a team to remove Ernemann. Well, you couldn't say it wasn't flattering.

"Precisely," Mac said. "What obstacle has Mr. Soo encountered on the last three occasions he tried to operate here? It is probable that, by now, he is giving a certain U.S. agent credit for more competence than he actually possesses; that he has an almost superstitious feeling about this man. At any rate, it is known that he planned to make certain that this individual would not live to interfere again."

I said, "Hell, that's too wild a coincidence, sir. You mean that Ernemann was collecting from three different clients for three simultaneous jobs?"

"Not at the start. It began, I gather, as a simple hit on

a Mexican general, paid for by one of his countrymen. This, of course, did not concern us. However, I learned that well after the Mexican contract had been arranged, Mr. Soo approached Ernemann and was told that the customary deposit would entitle him to a place on the list, but there would be a slight, unavoidable delay in dealing with his problem. Naturally, since information had already been received that Soo had plans in this direction, I was curious about whom he wanted killed. It took considerable investigation, but I found out. My next move, obviously, was to arange to have Mr. Ernemann eliminated during the course of his present engagement, before he could embark on the next one."

"Yes, obviously," I said. "I appreciate the thought, sir."

"We can't have contracts put out on our people," Mac said. "It shows a certain lack of respect, shall we say. Since you were an interested party, I considered using you in the front lines, but you were in need of some rest and therapy, remember? I did, however, advise the members of the primary team that you would be available for backup if needed. In the meantime, I understand, a certain person we won't name—as you seem to have decided for yourself; we have troubles enough without tackling a ruthless lady with millions at her disposal—had persuaded Ernemann to expand his Mexico operation slightly, for a substantial fee, even offering additional money to be used for the purpose of hampering the pursuit."

"Yes, I don't get that," I said. "If Ernemann was coming after me next, why did he try to frame me into jail where he wouldn't have been able to get at me?"

Mac smiled thinly. "It is pleasant to meet an American citizen with such touching faith in the inviolability of his nation's prisons, Eric. Anyway, I doubt that Ernemann really expected his little diversion to be effective in your case—as it turned out not to be. Suddenly you were there, close behind him; the man he'd contracted to dispose of next. Can you blame Mr. Ernemann for deciding to kill all his birds at once and collect for all of them?"

I said, "You've got to hand it to the guy, he didn't mind thinking big. He could have got rich on one night's work, if it had worked." I drew a long breath and said, "Well, I suppose I have to go after Soo next and see what he's up to."

Mac shook his head. "No. Someone else has that assignment. Your mind would not have been on it; and I think a certain French marquis, and a certain British ex-colonel, should be taught a small lesson, if it turns out to be justified. This hostage business must be discouraged. Find out exactly what happened to Norma, and then do whatever you consider appropriate by way of reprisal. You have a free hand as long as you are reasonably discreet."

"Thank you, sir," I said. "I appreciate—"

The telephone rang. Mac picked it up from the table beside him and held it out to me.

"Helm here," I said.

"I'm glad I finally caught you, old chap," said a familiar voice.

I hesitated, and glanced at Mac. "What can I do for you, Colonel Huntington?" I asked at last.

"For me?" He laughed. "Nothing, thank you very much. You have already done it—done me out of some very lucrative employment, for the second time. It's what I can do for you that concerns us now. Are you interested?"

"Of course."

"Guaymas. The Hotel Playa de Cortez. Room 212."

"I know the hotel," I said. "What will I find there?"

"I do not make war on women, old chap. Old-fashioned of me, what? I also do not make dangerous enemies unnecessarily; you never know, in this business, when some angry fellow will blow your head off simply because you trod on his toes when you could just as easily have walked around him. The Marquis was unhappy; he wanted blood, but the troops were mine, don't you know? Let's say that I'd rather have him for an enemy than you; he doesn't shoot quite so straight at five hundred meters. You'd have come after me, right?"

"Righto, old chap," I said. "I just received the orders."

"Now you are saved the trouble. She'll call in a few minutes and let you know she is safe and her collarbone is knitting well. Next time we meet, I expect a bottle of good Scotch. Cheers."

"Thanks," I said. "Just name your brand—"

I heard the click as the connection was broken. Mac was waiting expectantly. I looked at him, drawing a long breath.

I said, "Norma is at the Hotel Playa de Cortez, in Guaymas—that's in Sonora, Mexico. I gather she's in reasonable shape. So I guess you'd better figure out another job for me, sir."

He studied me for a moment, thoughtfully. When he spoke, his tone was severe: "I am sorry to see you taking your work so casually, Mr. Helm. Do you really consider that an acceptable finish to an assignment? When I send a man to discover what has happened to a missing agent, I do not expect to be put off with hearsay evidence gathered over the telephone from unreliable sources. I suggest you either return to the ranch for a course of intensive retraining, or complete your mission in a professional manner." He paused, and continued without expression: "My impression is that Guaymas is only a day's drive from here; and that the climate is very pleasant in winter."

It was.

The great MATT HELM suspense series—

Death of a Citizen	P3338	$1.25
The Wrecking Crew	P3336	$1.25
The Removers	P3337	$1.25
The Silencers	M3000	95¢
Murderers' Row	M2996	95¢
The Ambushers	M2998	95¢
The Shadowers	M2995	95¢
The Ravagers	P3339	$1.25
The Devastators	Q3512	$1.50
The Betrayers	P3291	$1.25
The Menacers	P3280	$1.25
The Interlopers	Q3498	$1.50
The Poisoners	P3244	$1.25
The Intriguers	P3379	$1.25
The Intimidators	Q3489	$1.50
The Terminators	P3214	$1.25
The Retaliators	1-3567-5	$1.50

"If you have a dozen thrillers at hand
and one is by Donald Hamilton, you can
either grab it at once or save it for
dessert."

—BOOK WORLD

From Fawcett Gold Medal . . .

Great Adventures in Reading

Fiction
THE BEST SELLERS
by Stephen Lewis   0-449-13538-1 $1.95

Mystery Suspense
THE MALPAS LEGACY
by Ariadne Pritchett   0-449-13539-X $1.25

THREE MOTIVES FOR MURDER
by Roy Winsor   0-449-13542-X $1.25

Non-fiction
HOW TO KNOW WHAT TO BELIEVE
by Harold Sherman   0-449-13540-3 $1.50

Romance
JEALOUS YESTERDAYS
by Marcia Miller   0-449-13541-1 $1.25

Humor
SEX ON SEX   0-449-13543-8 $1.25